SAPPHI(
Lesbian

By Lisa Rose Farrow

DEDICATION

These words are lovingly dedicated to all of those
seeking understanding. Especially dedicated
with love and kisses to Chastity Belden — the girl
who was different.

SAPPHIC PROMISE
Lesbian Submission

PREFACE. Chastity Belden

I have a lifelong friend by the name of Chastity
Belden. Chastity is, shall we say, different. I
learned everything I needed to know about
Chastity when we were in grade school.

The math teacher, a sturdy woman named Miss
Estelle who had been teaching math for
generations, most likely since Abraham Lincoln
had been in office, posed the following problem
to the group of young children.

*You have two oranges in a basket. I give you two
more and you put them in the basket. You take one
orange out of the basket. How many oranges do you
have?*

Chastity's hand immediately went up and the
teacher called on her. She proudly answered
"Four oranges". "No," the teacher said "Four
minus one leaves three". Chastity confidently
replied.

"No, *you* are wrong. Four. Three in the basket
and the one in your hand equals four."

The classroom burst out in laughter. Miss Estelle
wasn't laughing. Chastity was summarily sent to

the principal's office for smarting off to the teacher. We all heard her crying while the paddle was applied numerous times to her bottom.

You would think that would be a lesson well learned. But to this day Chastity insists that the correct answer is four.

She also says that her parents were hopeful when they named her Chastity. "Chastity" she says, "is more wishful thinking on their part than it is a lifestyle. I consider my name to be a mere suggestion that I choose to give little consideration to."

Chastity was the first girl who I ever kissed. Or I should say the first girl who kissed me. She taught me that kissing girls is different than kissing boys in a most delightful way.

That, my reader, is Chastity in a nutshell. This story is for her and is inspired by my loving relationship with her.

PROLOGUE. I Am Chastity

Hi my name is Chastity Belden. I believe that we are all different in our own special way. My father is a preacher and my mother is his loyal bookkeeper.

I attended college and obtained a degree in Business Administration because I wanted to be a financial advisor. I even have a hard earned license to practice my given profession.

At the same time I was in college my mother sent me to cosmetology night school. She thought that I could work in a salon, perhaps cutting hair or doing makeovers. I had no such interest but I attended the classes in the evenings essentially to please her.

It was there that I had my natural black hair dyed strawberry blonde and cropped short into a bob typically worn by older married women or girls working menial jobs such as a waitress or a maid. It was certainly not a style suitable for a young lady looking for love. My parents approved of the bland style even if I didn't.

My instructor said that girls with blonde hair get better tips. Mom said that boys like blonde hair better. I thought the color made me look and feel like a clueless airhead. I never thought of myself to be a blonde bimbo even if others thought that I was. Nevertheless I kept the color to please them both and often used the excuse that I was just a dumb blonde whenever I made a mistake or did something silly.

My father had different plans for me. He wanted the daughter of a minister to be the assistant bookkeeper for his wife. Even today I can't think of a more boring profession. I had more ambitious ideas than either of them regarding what I wanted to do with my life.

I suppose that my name was wishful thinking on the part of my father. Chastity? Really? It's okay for parents to dream. I have dreams too. I am my own woman and I am certainly not chaste.

That's how I found myself in this situation.

CHAPTER 1. A Kiss

It was only one act. I thought it unfair to be judged by it but in the house of a Minister that was all it took. My best friend Jill was moving out of town. All we did was kiss goodbye.

I'll admit that our kiss got somewhat out of hand. A peck on the lips turned into an open mouth goodbye that led to something that may have been perceived to be a forbidden make out session between two girls. At least that was what my parents thought it was when they came upon the scene.

Oh those soft kissable lips! They were angelic pedals sent from heaven. You would think that of all people a preacher would understand that.

I'll admit that sparks flew. For a brief moment I found myself thinking about a lifetime of intimate conversations, passionate cuddling and sharing a wardrobe with a woman who I loved. For me it was a magic moment that opened up possibilities that were supposed to be taboo. My parents didn't think so.

They called it a horrific forbidden act. I thought it to be more of a pleasant interlude that left me longing for more. I told them so. They disagreed. A long heated argument ensued. The daughter of a preacher can't be seen doing such things. Heaven forbid! They said that such displays would destroy their reputation and cost them their esteemed positions of reverence. Whatever that is.

I suppose that was the first time that I realized that I was attracted to other women. In fact I was *very* attracted to other women. I felt extremely confused by feelings that my gender said that I wasn't supposed to have.

My parents had kept me well-sheltered. I had never really been given a chance to explore my sexuality. It's not like I wanted to go to Burning Man or anything like that but I did want to explore those special feelings. Especially those prohibited feelings for another woman.

Anyway that's how I found myself standing in an airport with an overnight bag in one hand and my cell phone in the other. I was tired from the flight. I had been ushered out of my home so fast that I didn't have time to pack a change of clothes in the bag. So it only contained the minimum of basics for daily hygiene. The only clothes I had were those on my back.

Back home they had even taken me to the airport to be sure I left town. They picked the destination. I did not. Then they told me to have a good life and never to come back. I had no intention of ever doing so.

So there I was at my destination in an airport that I had never been to. There could be no going back. I didn't have the funds to do so even if I wanted to. It had been a long flight. Those meager possessions, plus a few dollars were all that I had to my name. The battery was fading on my cell but it had just enough juice to do a quick job hunt.

Help wanted. Lady's maid for a single woman. Room and board included. Respond to Miss Deanna Travers. Serious inquiry only.

I want to make something clear right from the onset. In spite of my ditzy blonde appearance it's not like I didn't have skills. I was well educated. It wasn't the work, or the wages. It was the fringe benefits that put me in the Uber and had me dropped off in front of the home of Miss Deanna Travers.

Unless you have been in a similar situation you may not realize that when you are homeless and alone in a strange town free room and board is

unbelievably appealing. Even if one must
become a domestic servant in order to obtain it.

Under such circumstance shelter from a storm is
the foremost thing on your mind. So even
though I had no experience working as a
domestic I thought that if free room and board
was included that I could easily fake it. After all I
had kept my room neat and tidy at home. At
least I had most of the time.

CHAPTER 2. Mirror Image

The home of Miss Travers was well off the beaten path. Like most persons of wealth apparently Miss Travers also liked the privacy that a country estate offers. Even though I wasn't wealthy I always thought that it would be nice to live in such seclusion. In a place like that I would be free to do whatever I pleased.

From the sweeping circular drive to the twin spires that towered above the edifice the home looked impressive. You could call it a mansion, a manor, a castle or a large estate. Pick your term. Whatever you choose to identify it with the place was one big whale of a home. It was certainly large enough to require a maid. It was maybe even large enough to require several maids. I thought it to be good fortune. I was sure to be hired. How could I miss? There seemed to be a dearth of applicants at the front door. In fact I was the only one.

I'm not sure if I was desperate, imagining things or just exhausted from the trip. When Miss Travers opened the front door I was taken aback by the stunningly attractive woman who presented herself.

She was impeccably dressed. She wore a black beaded evening gown that was slit down on one side enough to show plenty of leg. A daring look for any lady. I thought that she might be going out to the opera or another similar venue where the idea was to impress the other guests. I was wrong. I later learned that was how she dressed just to be around the house.

I couldn't help but notice her dazzling black hair. Her beautiful Cleopatra locks swept down to her shoulders framing her charming smile. Her hair was a stark contrast to my own straight blonde bob style. My own plain look was not stylish in any way. I had always been told to wear my hair that way so that my tempting charms wouldn't entice the boys to do something that I might regret later. Of course the only thing I ever regretted was not enticing the boys to do whatever they wanted with me. I doubt that I would have regretted that.

Miss Travers was dressed to captivate any male who might find himself in her orbit. There was no question about that. Even her musky perfume bid males to come her way. I guess she thought that a male might drop in out of the blue sky at any moment so she wanted to be prepared.

There was something else about her aside from her apparent desperate attempt at male seduction that struck me. The thing is that it was immediately noticeable to me that aside from her bounty of delightful black Cleopatra styled hair Deanna Travers was a mirror image of *me*. It was odd. It was like looking in a magical mirror and seeing yourself only you were rich so you were dressed differently in the reflection. She clearly had a bounty of clothing riches while I was dressed in the equivalent of peasant rags.

She was a true beauty who certainly could turn heads. She had the same trim figure, the same breasts, the same legs that I was so proud of, very kissable pouty lips and a smile that could dazzle anyone. She could even dazzle me. I was immediately smitten — taken by her mere presence.

I could imagine myself styled with that beautiful head of hair, wearing a beaded gown and looking just like her. My gown would be a stunning blue though because that's my favorite color. There was no doubt about it we could be twins except for her fancy trimmings. In my mind that was the only difference between us. She was a perfect identical sister if ever there was one. We were like peas in a pod in every way. Or so I thought.

Oddly I saw no hint of recognition whatsoever from Miss Travers. I suppose that she only viewed me to be a Craigslist respondent to her brief ad and no more than that. Perhaps it was because she was wearing a beautiful dress that flattered her every curve while I was in faded jeans and a cheap tank top. I'm sorry to say that's what I had on when I was summarily dismissed at the airport like yesterday's dirty laundry.

I suppose that's why she looked at me like I *was* yesterday's dirty laundry.

"Whatever are you doing on my front porch young lady? Whatever you are selling I don't want any. Go away."

I had never been spoken to like that before. A preacher's daughter is always treated with respect. At least I had been. She couldn't have been more condescending had she tried to be.

"I'm Miss Chastity Belden. I called earlier for the maid position."

"Oh, I suppose that you are the one."

I wish she hadn't put it that way. It was a painful reminder. When I was inquiring on the position my cell phone had been disconnected mid-sentence. There had still been a wisp of battery life left but that was not the problem. Apparently being banished out of town meant no more freeloading with cell service either. Fortunately I had been given Miss Travers's address before the line went dead and before, in a less than womanly fit of anger, I had hurled the phone into the trash. I hadn't even had time to give her my name.

She looked me up and down like I was an item featured in a grocery store meat counter.

"Come in dear and tell me what you have to offer me though I doubt it to be much of anything."

That was my introduction to my new life in the service of Miss Deanna Travers. It only took an hour after that before she pronounced that since she had no other applicants that she would have to settle for me.

I was hired.

CHAPTER 3. Cheap French Harlot

Miss Travers made it immediately clear that I was not acceptable to her in the condition that I was in. She insisted upon sprucing me up — her words not mine — before I could be put to work.

She immediately showed me to my new quarters — a tiny bedroom in the farthest reaches of the home back behind the kitchen that had its own little private bath. There I received my first inclination of what was in store for me in the service of Miss Travers.

She insisted that I disrobe in front of her. She said that she wanted to see what she had to work with. I did so reluctantly even though disrobing in the presence of a woman shouldn't have bothered me. Yet there was something in her eyes that made me feel uneasy.

She seemed far too interested in my appearance. She stared at me with interest. You might even say that she was ogling me. I could swear that she was checking me out. Not the way an employer might but rather in the manner that an interested lover might. Could it be that she had a sexual interest in me? Then I convinced myself that I was only imagining that. Perhaps she realized our likeness. She stared at me stoically while I stripped down to my panties. Then she insisted that those go too.

She shook her head in disapproval.

"A girl should be shaved down there. You know, for cleanliness. You are to remove that unsightly brush in the bath. Do not come out until it is gone."

I thought it rather brazen for an employer to make such a comment. But under the circumstances I was forgiving. Fortunately I had thought of shaving my legs and had packed more than enough items to get the job done. I thought it a strange request for an employer to demand I shave my love nest but she was after all the boss. Besides I would have a bed to sleep in that night so I wasn't about to argue with her.

I felt her eyes follow me into the bathroom. I quickly closed the door to obtain a respectable measure of decency. She had seen me naked but I wasn't about to let her watch me bathe. Of course after a quick soak and careful work with my razor I had no choice but to go back out into the room wearing nothing but a towel. There she sat on the bed patiently waiting for me.

My jeans and tank top were nowhere to be found. Instead she was holding up a garter belt in one hand and stockings in the other. On the bed next to her was a pair of thong panties and a push up bra.

The towel only covered my breasts. I was painfully aware of the itching between my legs from shaving and what felt like an unfamiliar cool breeze down there.

Her eyes went straight to my exposed womanhood and a smile broadened her face.

"That's much better dear. I think you'll enjoy the look and feel of that. I insist that you keep yourself shaved down there for the duration of your employment. Failure to do so will result in immediate dismissal. Understand?"

I nodded my head yes. It was such a strange request. I wondered how she would ever enforce it. I didn't have time to ask.

"Miss Belden, when I give you an order you are to acknowledge it properly. I expect formality from my maid not to mention strict obedience. Yes Miss Travers was in order just now."

"Yes Miss Travers."

"That's much better. I'll teach you to curtsy later."

"Now get dressed girl."

Apparently she intended to watch. I thought her to be a voyeur who relished the power of ordering her naked servant to dress. So I quickly pulled on the garter belt, fastened the stockings, pulled up the panties and clipped on the bra while she casually observed every movement.

The garments were a bawdy tease. I had never worn stockings before. Mom always said that nice girls wore pantyhose and that stockings were for streetwalkers and showgirls. The push up bra made my breasts more prominent. I casually wondered to myself why a maid would wear such things.

I had never worn a thong before. The satin panty was gently caressing my freshly shaved pubes while simultaneously nestling itself in the crack of my buttocks. It was downright sinful but pleasing nonetheless. The push-up bra made my breasts feel like giant balloons that were prominently on display.

Miss Travers licked her lips in proud approval. Then she opened the closet door and to my surprise it was filled with French maid uniforms. My first thought was that such attire would make me feel rather slutty to wear. I wondered why she had such clothing in her home and I pondered how they must have got there. I guess I should have inquired about the previous maid before I took the job.

Miss Travers watched while I slipped into the uniform. It was a short black dress that zipped up the back with white lace at the sleeves and neck. When I say *short* I mean *short* beyond reason. Even standing straight up the bottom of my buttocks had to be sinfully visible. A fancy lace cap and a lace apron completed the tawdry ensemble. After I put on the heels that accompanied the attire I felt like a cheap French harlot. I couldn't believe that she expected me to work in an outfit like that.

Again Miss Travers licked her lips and pronounced that it was time to put me to work.

CHAPTER 4. To Work

There was much to be done in the sizeable home of Miss Travers. After my long day I wanted to relax but instead Miss Travers had me hard at work for the duration of the day. She carefully watched me with a critical eye while I vacuumed, dusted and attacked a pile of laundry that had clearly been accumulating for quite a while.

I learned that she wore evening gowns every day because there was a mountain of them that needed to be either laundered or sent out for cleaning. Her lingerie was mostly delicate lace and needed to be hand washed and line dried. So while she had a washing machine for her lingerie it was essentially useless for the task at hand.

At dusk I found myself out in the large backyard bringing her unmentionables down from the line and putting them into the laundry basket. When I came into the house that evening Miss Travers was waiting for me. She was so pleased with my work that she surprised me with a big wet kiss flush on my lips.

CHAPTER 5. Companionship

Miss Travers lived alone. It didn't take too long before I realized that she was looking for more than just a housemaid. Over the weeks I learned that she was lonely and in desperate need of companionship. So we conversed while she would take her meals. I would stand at attention like the dutiful maid while she would chatter away like a teenage girl. Other times she would stand over me while I worked supervising while we talked.

I learned all about her. She came into her wealth the old fashioned way — inheritance. Her parents had a misfortunate automobile accident when she was an infant so she had been raised by her rather eccentric grandfather.

Let me give you an idea of how innocent Miss Travers apparently was. She told me how her grandfather had made his fortune programming top secret software for the Navy back in the 1980's. She said that he had worked on a classified project called Commodore 64 writing all sorts of computer code. She said she didn't know if he worked on Commodore 1 thru 63 but she was sure that he had worked on Commodore 64.

The poor girl thought that Commodore was a reference to the Navy. Can you believe it? Of course she was referring to the original home computer built for the masses. Her grandfather had written long forgotten obscure programs that had sold by the millions but she didn't seem to grasp that. Perhaps that explained the unusual terms of her inheritance.

There were strict requirements for her inheritance. Violation of any of the requirements meant forfeiture of her home and all of her money.

She received a small monthly allowance for expenses. A friend of her grandfather named Miss Trish Anne Billingham acted like a financial advisor and administered the fortune in investment accounts that were held in her name. But she didn't know where the funds were held, only that Miss Billingham knew everything and that it was at the discretion of Miss Billingham how much to give her and when to give her full access.

She was required to visit the Miss Billingham every month. It was a task that she loathed because she had no interests whatsoever in financial dealings.

She was also required to attend meetings every month of The Queen's Tea Society — a group of wealthy women who were financially savvy and who were intent on teaching Miss Travers everything about being a wealthy heiress. The head of the society, one Miss Isabella Ellsworth held the deed to her home and should Miss Travers not appear as required it was her instruction to sell the home right out from under her. It was also at the discretion of Miss Ellsworth as to when to relinquish the deed.

The two meetings were staggered so that every two weeks Miss Travers had to attend one meeting or the other. That made it clear that the estate had been set up to be a learning experience for Miss Travers. Unfortunately she had no interest in learning so she was stuck into the boring routine.

The result was that Miss Travers was not a happy woman. She longed to be free of Miss Billingham and to be rid of the prudish women who gathered to drink tea. She wanted to live a life free of mandatory meetings and the accompanied burdens.

It was one evening while she ate her dinner that she shared her secret with me.

CHAPTER 6. Envy

"I envy you Chastity. I envy your life and I envy the freedom that you have. I once thought of running away and becoming a maid myself. You are living the life that I've always desired."

I couldn't believe what I was hearing. The woman who had everything wanted to be like me! She said it with such sincerity I knew that she meant it. Then something occurred to me.

"Miss Travers, the uniforms that are in my bedroom. There was no maid here before me was there?

"No there wasn't."

"Did you buy them for yourself?"

She gave me a little smile.

"You've guessed my secret. I once planned to leave this place and go to work like a common maid."

"Why didn't you go?"

"I worried that I might change my mind later. If I left then I would lose everything. Then I would be broke. I'm not trained to do anything really. I was always well taken care of. I had hoped to find an employer with a sexual interest in me so that I could keep a position."

At that moment I realized that Deanna needed my sympathy. I came over and stood behind her and lightly stroked her hair. She took my hand and kissed it. Then she started to cry.

"Oh Chastity you're so *perfect.*"

I hardly knew what to say. Finally the words came to me.

"No, I'm not perfect Miss Travers. *You* are perfect. You have everything a girl could possibly desire."

She turned to look me in the eyes. For the first time I realized what I was seeing in her. Those were *bedroom* eyes.

"I don't have everything. There is someone else who I desire."

I had seen that look before and heard those words before. I remembered Jill and how that kiss had felt. It was of course a forbidden kiss. I guess that's what made it so special.

My mouth opened but no words came out. I realized that I may have unintentionally led her on.

"You don't have to say anything dear. I know that you want me too. I could see it in your eyes the moment you stepped in the house."

"But we shouldn't…"

"No we shouldn't. An employer and her maid! What a scandal! It would be wrong."

She reached under my dress and her hand gently stroked my satin panties. A shiver of delight shook my body.

"Yes…I mean no…it would be wrong…"

"You're right. I wouldn't think to do so."

She took her hand away. I was disappointed. She pouted.

"See me to my chambers. I've had enough for today."

She stood up and walked off in a huff. I hurried to catch up with her while she quickly went up the stairs to the second floor where the bedrooms were. She stood next to her bed and snarled a command.

"Fetch me a nightgown girl and hang it next to the tub."

It was an order with a mean tone to it. I quickly went to her closet and pulled out one of her many fabulous night gowns.

Typically after that she would then dismiss me for the day. This evening would be different.

"I need a bath. Draw me a bubble bath girl. Run the water for me and get back here."

I turned the water on in her luxurious private bath. While the tub filled I came back to Miss Travers.

"Help me undress girl."

My hands shook while I fumbled with her gown. When I unzipped her it fell to the floor and she stepped out of it. I had seen her lingerie before but only in the laundry. Her body filled out the lace like a shapely goddess. Her legs were perfect in their shimmering stockings.

"Are you going to gawk at me or help me undress?"

I realized that I had been staring at her beauty. How could I not? I quickly helped her out of her underclothes. She was naked when she casually walked towards the tub.

"Come with me girl."

I followed her and she stood naked by the tub while I tested the water for temperature. I found it to be perfect so I turned off the faucet. I gently held her hand while she gracefully stepped in and then lowered herself into the bubbles. I took a step to leave but she stopped me.

"You are to stay here. I'll need you to towel me off later."

"Yes Miss Travers."

CHAPTER 7. Masturbation Fantasy

It seemed like she soaked for hours. I stood at attention trying not to glance at her body. I tried hard not to peek at her but I couldn't resist. I kept looking at her out of the corner of my eye even though she was mostly covered with fluffy bubbles.

It wasn't until I heard a soft moan that I realized that things had changed beneath the water. Miss Travers had closed her eyes. With her face flushed she seemed to be fingering herself into an excited frenzy. She tipped her head back and bucked and moaned in ecstatic pleasure.

I stayed at attention while her animal squeals escalated into a passionate orgasmic scream of pleasure followed by a soft whimper of quenched satisfaction. Miss Travers had shamelessly masturbated herself without any concern whatsoever for my presence!

After a few moments to compose herself she calmly asked for a towel. Then she stepped out of the tub into the soft dry embrace that I held out for her. After I toweled her dry I helped her into her nightgown.

Once she was dressed she gently touched the front of my satin panties.

"Oh my. You're damp down there. Perhaps you have more interest in me than you let on to. I can fix that. Come with me girl."

She led me back into the bedroom. Then I offered no resistance while she had me lay back on her bed. She slid my thong off and dropped it on the floor. I held still with anticipation of certain sexual release while she searched a drawer. Finally she pulled out a device that at first I didn't recognize.

When she came closer I realized that she had a metal chastity belt in her hand. It was a diabolical throwback to a medieval time when women needed the ultimate in impenetrable personal protection. When she started to put me into it I tried to kick and squirm away but my effort was futile. Perhaps I didn't really want to resist whatever plan she had in mind for me because I finally gave in to her.

Miss Travers was fully intent upon putting me into a chastity belt and I didn't have the will to stop her. I was no match for her insistence. Even though I had struggled the belt found its place. When she was finished she tugged the belt tight into my crotch and locked it in place. I was sexually at her mercy restrained like I was in my first chastity belt.

"Since you have no interest in me yet you are so wet I thought it best to protect you from yourself. You will wear the chastity belt until I decide to remove it. You'll have to ask to use the ladies room and I will supervise to make sure that you don't attempt to pleasure yourself."

She put the distinctive gold chain that the key to my sex was attached to around her neck. Then she smiled at me.

"That's enough for today girl, you're dismissed."

I couldn't believe it. My slit was dripping wet beneath the metallic restraint and definitely in urgent need of attention. There was no relief that night for me. There couldn't be. There wasn't any sleep for me either.

The next morning Miss Travers removed my chastity belt and watched me while I took care of my needs and then bathed. When I stepped out of the tub I was immediately locked back into the device. She told me to put my uniform on and then get to work.

CHAPTER 8. Chastity Living

It was not just the belt that was distracting. I found the degradation of my restrained position to be erotic. With my pubes shaved and the belt tight in my crotch against my clitoris I was in a constant state of unfulfilled arousal.

Miss Travers seemed indifferent to my situation. She ordered me about like the maid servant that I was but my mind was not on my work. Instead it was fixated on the tender throbbing that was going on underneath my metal prison.

I struggled attired with the device for a full week until I couldn't take it anymore. I thought I was going to go insane with lust. I had to do whatever it took to have the contraption removed from covering my most sacred place.

I tapped on the door to her office where she was seated behind a big mahogany desk. She told me to enter and I walked in. I gave her my obligatory curtsy before I spoke.

"Please Miss Travers, may I have a word."

"Why yes maid Chastity, what seems to be the problem?"

She knew darn well what the problem was but she wasn't about to admit it.

"Miss Travers if I may, could you please remove my chastity belt? I beg of you to show me mercy."

She stood up from her chair and walked over to me. She positioned herself just inches away from me while she spoke.

"I might be persuaded to remove it but I must ask first. What's in it for me?"

At that point I didn't need any encouragement. I leaned forward and my tongue dove deep inside her mouth in a desperate erotic kiss. I felt her gentle hands cup my buttocks pulling me forward against a firm thigh. She returned my kiss with a welcome intertwining of our tongues. I couldn't help myself. I thought it wise for a girl imprisoned in chastity to encourage her key holder.

"Oh, yes, please, yesss, ohhh yes!"

I felt a dampness growing and my nipples hardening. How could this feel so good? It wasn't supposed to feel like that but it did. At that moment I wanted Miss Travers more than anything else in the world. I didn't think that I was a lesbian, but maybe I was. If I had to be a lesbian in order to have Miss Travers than I most certainly *was* a lesbian.

She pushed me away.

"You've not learned your lesson just yet maid Chastity. When I see you naked in my bedchambers than that's when I'll know that you're ready. Until then you are dismissed!"

I couldn't believe it. She turned away and sat back down behind her desk and was immediately engrossed in some kind of paperwork. I had gotten a taste of her but her sweet flavor was not enough for me. I wanted the rest of her too.

I resumed my duties. If Miss Travers was going to be a tease than I could be a tease too. At least I could be until that evening.

CHAPTER 9. Bedroom Frolic

I heard Miss Travers calling my name but I wasn't about to answer her. Instead I stayed in position. I was on her bed naked with the exception of the chastity belt with my legs spread wide apart. I could only hope that when she saw me in such an inviting position that she would have mercy on such a tawdry maid.

I had decided that I would give in to my desires. I didn't care what other people might think. Screw them! I was Chastity Belden and only I knew what was best for me. What could possibly go wrong with such thinking?

Of course I still had a touch of trepidation. I was reminded of a quote from comedian Iliza Shlesinger who once said *You know what happened the last time a group of women said, Screw it, we don't care what you think? They were hung as witches!*

That of course was a worst case scenario and was certainly not applicable in this situation. At least I hoped so. With that I disregarded my guilt feelings and checked to make sure that I was positioned enticingly in the center of the bed.

When she finally came into to the bedroom she smiled at the scene that I presented for her but she did not speak a word. Instead our eyes locked while she slowly undressed herself. Finally she stood naked at the foot of the bed wearing only the chain with the key to my lust dangling from her neck.

I didn't move while she slowly unlocked and removed my chastity belt. All I could hear was my heart pounding in my ears. Then Deanna stretched out next to me and her hand gently caressed the inside of my thigh.

Deanna's fingers then slid down to my wetness and then one finger teased at my clitoris. I let out a soft compliant moan. She knew just how to excite me with her feminine touch and I wasn't about to resist her in any way. I was immersed in the fragrance of her perfume and the soft caress that teased my whole body. Soon we were intertwined pelvis to pelvis, vulva to vulva in a passionate frenzy of heart thumping sex.

We shamelessly squirmed, shrieked, writhed and reared in wondrous pleasure each feeding on the magnificent femininity of the other. We unapologetically fingered, nibbled, licked and fucked each other in a frenzy of sex until we both rested panting on the bed in sensual exhaustion.

It had been a forbidden dance that only two women could experience. It was pure bliss.

CHAPTER 10. Aftermath

We were too exhausted from the effort for
another delightful interlude. Instead we lay back
in satiated ecstasy still naked and cuddling
together in an intimate embrace. I would have
been satisfied to enjoy the bliss in silence but
Miss Travers wanted to talk. She whispered in
my ear.

"I've always wanted to do that."

"You've never…"

"No. I was a virgin."

"Me too."

There were a few moments of silence while the
weight of what had happened settled on us. I felt
a flash of sinful guilt but only for a moment. It
had been far too heavenly to be anything other
than good. Finally she broke the quiet.

"Why haven't you had sex before?"

"I never met a boy who excited me enough."

"What about girls?"

"My parents wouldn't have understood. There was a girl named Jill but I got into big trouble with her with just a kiss so things never progressed too far. Oh that one kiss! It was so divine. You know girls taste different than boys."

"I know."

"What about you?"

"I'm not the type to initiate that sort of thing…"

I couldn't believe what I was hearing. She certainly didn't seem to be the virginal type.

"What do you mean not the type? Deanna you pinned me to the bed and you practically raped me. Don't tell me that you're not the type. I don't believe you."

"Well I'm not."

I was confused.

"Okay then what type *are* you?"

I could tell that she was embarrassed. But after the intimacy that we had shared I guess she felt that she could let somebody in on her secret.

"I've always wanted to feel the pleasure of another woman. I always dreamed that somebody would approach me but it never happened. I have a desire for Sapphic love but also for brazen raw sex. Have you ever just wanted to be tied up and forced to have an orgasm? Just the thought of it can make me..."

"Deanna I think I get the picture."

"Do you? Is there something wrong with me? I want to be *taken*. I even bought those maid uniforms for myself because the thought of wearing them excited me. I thought that if I exhibited myself to a woman in them that she would desire me. I want sex so bad but my dream is to have a *woman* force me to have sex with her. What am I to do?"

I didn't answer her. Instead I just held her tight. I knew that she was leading me on. She was begging me for a sexual relationship in her own inhibited way. I didn't want to rush into anything. I decided that I would give it thought. What we had was splendid unabashed sex and for the moment I wanted to keep it at that. We slept together naked that night in each other's embrace.

That next morning I crept out of Deanna's bedroom before she woke up. I went down to my quarters, put my uniform on and went back to work preparing her breakfast.

When Deanna came down from her bedroom wearing a modest evening gown she seemed so embarrassed by what she had done the day before. She didn't say a word about it instead treating me like nothing at all had happened.

Later that morning she went off to see Miss Billingham while I continued with my domestic chores. There were dishes to wash and floors to mop so I dove right in. Hours later she came back woefully despondent and she immediately began to grumble.

"I can't take it anymore. That woman will drive me insane. She dwells on stocks, bonds, dividends and other things that I have no knowledge of. All we do is sit and talk business. That's it, I'm just going to walk away."

"What will you do with yourself?"

"I don't know. I guess I'll just starve myself."

It was that moment when the faint flicker of an idea crossed my mind. I decided to think about it and nurture the concept before I did anything rash and act on my impulse.

CHAPTER 11. The Diary

The custom of keeping a diary is so quaint. These days those keeping a written record of their life and of their secret ambitions usually choose to do so on a computer. That's why I was so surprised the morning when I accidently discovered where Deanna kept her personal diary.

I was putting away her clean panties when I saw it. I was reorganizing her undies into a neat arrangement sorted by style and color and there it was right under a pink lace thong.

Even though her diary was hidden in her panty drawer and was meant to be kept personal I just had to read it. How could I not? Isn't that what everybody does when they come across someone else's diary?

Her inner thoughts were much different than the Deanna that she projected. I was so taken by the sensuality of her writing that over several days I read the whole diary cover to cover. I read about a shy reserved woman who was afraid to show her true self. Her attempts at being the strict Mistress of the Manor were a façade. Her authoritative actions were simply efforts to conceal her inner feelings.

Of most interest and of amusing surprise were her three secret desires. They formed a recurring pattern throughout her diary. One revelation was her true feelings for Miss Isabella Ellsworth. Contrary to what she had told me it was clearly apparent that Deanna was smitten with the woman and that she yearned for a sexual encounter.

It was also equally apparent that she was far too shy to approach the more mature woman for fear of rejection. While Miss Ellsworth had occasionally teased Deanna neither Miss Ellsworth's intentions nor her orientation were clear to Deanna.

She wrote quite often about a possible interlude with Miss Ellsworth.

I so want to be tutored in the fine art of Sapphic love by Miss Ellsworth. I long for a strict authoritative woman like her to take me to heights that I can't imagine. I yearn to be taken forcibly and taught all forms of sexual debauchery and to be compelled to endure erotic lessons in sexual interlude that I can't possibly conceive of. I lust for such wickedness and am often wet at the mere thought of it.

Another revelation was her adorable desire to be sensually spanked. Not a love tap mind you, but a downright bare-bottom paddling by the hand of a strict authoritative woman.

I am such a naughty girl to desire the love nest of another woman. My wanton desire for shameless sex will be the end of me. I have no desire for male companionship my desire is only for the love and touch of a beautiful woman. I deserve to be spanked like an errant child for my scandalous cravings. I would love to be disciplined like that though it would only add to my depravity for I am excited at the idea.

The final common thread was the very best of all.

I don't know why but I yearn to be of service to a lady. To become a lady's personal maid is the most exciting thought imaginable. I lust to be put in uniform and to be turned into a mere servant at the beck and call of another woman. To do so would be heaven and I routinely masturbate myself while thinking of how absolutely delightful it would be.

If her sexual orientation wasn't consciously clear to Deanna it sure was clear to me. Deanna was a true submissive with obvious Lesbian desires and far too shy to do anything about it. The quandary left her frustrated because she was only able to share her desires privately with her diary.

I found it odd that a woman could be so excited about such humiliating fantasies but I knew that I had to act upon them.

I had always thought of myself to be the traditional docile female type. I had fantasies that were similar to those I was reading in her diary but I too had never acted upon them. They were such scandalous thoughts! But for some reason reading about her submissive desires seemed to awaken my own desire to dominant her in every way.

The last entry in her diary was most riveting. She had already made a notation regarding the previous evening.

I hired a lovely woman to be my maid. I was taken by her beauty the moment I feasted my eyes on her. I couldn't resist myself – I've already been in bed with her. Am I wrong to do that? Absolutely not! I fear that I won't be able to resist her charms. She was so sweet and my orgasm was so blissful that surely I must have her again.

Naturally I put her diary carefully back where I found it because I didn't want her to know that I had seen it.

CHAPTER 12. The Plan

A couple of months had gone by since my discovery of Deanna's diary. I poured over every daily entry when she was not close enough to come upon me. In the interim Deanna had proven to be true to the shy girl who was portrayed in her book. Despite her sideways glances at me she made no further attempt to get cozy with me. Clearly she was waiting for me to make a move.

I had also taken the opportunity to explore the manor. She had been honest in her diary about her sexual taste and her home reflected it. One of the guest rooms was loaded with items of a sexual nature—none of which I had ever seen her use.

In the guest room there was a giant four poster bed with a large mirror suspended above it. There was a full length wall mirror at the foot of the bed. I could imagine Deanna gazing at herself while fantasizing and masturbating herself into a delightful orgasm.

The closet was filled with leather garments suitable for a Dominatrix. I found paddles, floggers, whips, chains, strapon devices and dildos in the dresser drawers. In that room everything in it was apparently just used for enhancing sexual pleasures. It was a veritable dungeon of sexual toys just waiting to be put to good use by the woman of Deanna's dreams.

Of course I had no idea how to use any of that. A preacher's daughter does not usually get exposed to such things. At least I didn't know how to make use of those decadent items at first. But after a bit of research I knew better. Exploring your sexuality can have many benefits. Since I had arrived I had learned quite a bit about sexual domination and sexual submission. The Internet can be quite handy for covertly acquiring such information.

Finally one morning I decided to make my move. I had taken out a sheer pink sheath dress for her that day and it clung to her shapely body revealing every inch of her charming features. After I served her breakfast I decided that it was time for me to take action.

"Deanna, I have an idea. Come with me."

I led her up to the guest room. She was quite shy about entering but I took her by the hand and led her in. There we stood in front of a full length mirror. I could see that she was quite

43

embarrassed that I had even found her secret room. A girl's sexuality is supposed to be a carefully guarded secret. Her secret was out and I was about to exploit it. Her face was flushed a deep red.

My hair had grown out since I had been employed and I had been wearing it up to keep it out of the way when I was working. I took the clips out of my hair and with a shake of my head let it fall down to my shoulders. It gave me the same classic Cleopatra look that Deanna had only I was blonde in contrast to her raven black head of hair. The two of us stood there looking at ourselves in the mirror.

"Deanna do you notice any resemblance?"

Her mouth gaped open.

"I never realized it! How could I have not seen that? Other than our hair color we could be twins!"

"The uniform does that to girls. A maid in uniform is just a servant. Nobody pays any attention to her even if she *has* been bedded."

"I'm so sorry…"

"Don't be. Because things are going to change around here starting right now."

"What do you mean by that?"

I mean that starting today we are going to change places. I'm going to become Miss Deanna Travers Mistress of the Manor and you are going to become Miss Chastity Belden my domestic maid."

I knew immediately that I had her. I knew her better than she knew herself. She squirmed a bit and fidgeted with her hands while she replied.

"That's nonsense. You can't make me a maid in my own household."

"Oh yes I can. You want it and you know it."

"I really don't think so…"

"Oh you will. I'll bet that you're already wet just imagining how delightful it would be to become maid Chastity and to work for me like a common servant."

"That's nonsense."

She said it so meekly that I knew that I had won.

"Lift your dress for me. I think that I'll find you so excited that you can hardly wait."

"What do you mean? I'll do no such thing! I'll not lift my dress for you!"

I smiled. That was exactly what I expected her to say.

"If you don't agree to do my bidding I'll have to give you a spanking on that cute bottom of yours."

"You wouldn't dare! You can't do that! You're just the maid!"

I went over to the dresser. I had placed a strapon that I had found in there over a leather paddle. I put the strapon on top of the dresser. I wanted her to see it so that she could imagine how I might use it on her. Then I took out the wooden paddle that I had placed underneath it. I turned to face her and again I could see that I had already won. Her eyes betrayed her in a manner that I knew would make her mine.

I glared at her with the most commanding look that I could summon.

"Lift your dress up for me Deanna."

"This is so silly. I've never…"

To my delight she started to struggle with the nylon sheath. It was so tight that she had to wiggle in order to raise it up past her hips.

I kept the paddle in my left hand while I moved closer. There was really no need for an inspection. Her erect nipples were clearly showing through her nylon sheath. The fragrant scent of her sex was already evident. Plus I could see that her nylon thong panties were already moist with arousal. None of that mattered though because I wanted to be sure of her total surrender.

"Panties down dear. I need to feel if you have been telling me the truth."

She was *so* indignant it was laughable. If she was so outraged than why was she obeying me? The answer was quite obvious. I had discovered her sexual desire to be dominated and I was exploiting it.

Surely she knew the moist condition of her love nest. Aroused the way that she was how could she not? In a move of total capitulation to my dominance she dropped her panties revealing her glistening shaved privates.

I doubt a woman other than a true submissive could have lowered herself to such humiliation. It was such an indignity for such a supposedly refined lady! She had lifted her dress and lowered her panties for me like she was no more than a common street harlot. There she was, the Mistress of the Manor, shamefully exposing herself to her maid for vaginal inspection.

I gently slid a finger inside of her. She was so hot and well lubricated that there could be no mistaking her intense desire. Just for fun I traced a little circle around her clitoris with my thumb. She let out a lewd gasp at the stimulation.

"Oh yes my dear. Your clitty betrays you. I can see that you want to become my maid and so my maid you will become."

"Oh yessss…"

"But first you lied to me. You said that you did not desire to become my maid. I can certainly tell that is not the case. I'll have to punish you for that."

My thumb made another tiny little circle.

"Oh nooo…"

I could tell that there was no conviction in that aroused response. She may well have just said that she surrendered to me. I whispered back to her.

"Oh yes dear."

CHAPTER 13. Meek Surrender

It didn't take much to put her over my lap. Deanna had meekly yielded to my bidding. Her willpower had melted away with the simple order to go over my knees.

I'm not ashamed to say that my heart fluttered and I felt a dampness growing in my panties when I put Deanna into the spanking position. How could I not feel powerful putting the Mistress of the Manor in her fine gown over my knee like she was an errant child?

While I carefully positioned her for the paddle she moaned in lewd expectation. I knew immediately that my plan would work. Emboldened I unceremoniously yanked her dress up well above her waist just to show her who was now going to be in charge.

I fingered her slit only to find her fluids gushing in willful anticipation. Then with a swift stroke of the paddle I smacked her rear with the best force of dominant authority that I could muster. Initially she squealed in protest at the force of the blow but after a couple of more strokes were administered her tone softened into a complaint whimper.

I had to put her in her place so I continued to spank her like she was a deserving naughty child. I lectured her telling her how shameful it was of her to have desires for other women and not to act on them. I told her that she was a slut who needed a spanking for not admitting that she wanted to be my maid.

She made no further effort to protest. Instead she only made moans of pleasure while writhing in submissive ecstasy. Deanna had waited a lifetime to fulfill her punishment fantasy and I made sure to fully indulge her in it.

When my arm tired from applying the discipline I put the paddle down and reached down past her reddened buttocks to assure myself of her consent. She was dripping wet from her willful submission. Her love nest had gushed fluids onto my stockings in tawdry approval. I had won.

When Deanna stood up her eyes were glazed over in erotic pleasure. I told her to give me her stockings and to remove her dress. She made absolutely no effort to resist my orders. She was only left with a lace bra for modesty. It was all far too easy.

There was a vanity in the room with a large mirror on it and I led her over to it and had her sit. She then watched herself in the mirror staring in complete capitulation while I took shears and styled her hair into a neat short bob. When I finished with her there were tufts of black hair on the floor and she had the same practical style that I had worn when I had first arrived at the mansion seeking employment from her.

It was a cut I had learned at night school. It was certainly not stylish enough for a wealthy Mistress of the Manor expecting callers but it was perfect for a lowly servant. With her hair out of the way she would be able to concentrate on her work like a proper maid would.

I gave her a box of blonde hair color. It was one of the few things that I had managed to pack before I left home.

"You are to return to the servant's quarters and dye your hair. Prepare yourself for your new career. Tomorrow you will report for duty in full uniform. The first thing you are to do in the morning is to clean up all of this hair. You've made quite a mess."

She stood up to leave.

"Just so you fully understand the situation let me be clear. Starting this instant I am taking your place. From now on you will address me as Miss Travers for I will in fact be Miss Deanna Travers. You, on the other hand, are taking my place. You will respond to maid Chastity Belden because you will in fact be my maid servant.

Your home, your wealth and your possessions now belong to me. You will stay in the maid's quarters where your own belongings are to be kept. I expect you to be in your maid uniform at all times. Do you understand me girl?"

I couldn't have sounded more condescending had I tried. She was such a submissive thing that she seemingly could not help herself. She was floundering in the juices of her own sex. She could not summon the will to resist the shameful lust of submitting to her hired maid.

Much to her liking and in fulfillment of her lifelong dream she had been dominated by a woman. Another woman had spanked her, disrobed her, sheared her locks and for the grand finale was then going to strip her of everything she owned. Her own secret desire for sexual humiliation had made it all possible for me. She was so excited by it all that she could only speak through trembling lips.

"Yes…Miss…Travers."

"You are dismissed."

"Thank you Miss Travers."

She turned to leave. My eyes settled on her swaying rear still reddened by the persuasion of the paddle. I couldn't help but feel pleased with myself. This was going to be fun.

CHAPTER 14. Reporting For Duty

My new blonde maid reported for duty as instructed that next morning. I have to admit that she was a delightful temptation in her French maid uniform. From behind she flashed a bit of her rear with her every move. I could see that her bottom was still faintly pink from the previous day's thrashing.

I put her to work washing the marble tile in the entrance foyer. It was the most humiliating job that I could think of for her to do. I had certainly put her in her place. I was wearing the same evening gown that she had worn the previous day just to show her that the exchange of roles had really taken place. I stood over her with my arms folded so that I could strictly supervise her work.

She looked so humbled down on her hands and knees polishing the floor tiles. Her dress was so short that her panties were in full view while she toiled away. It would be such an embarrassment for her if anyone she knew could see her degraded in such a manner. But it was what she wanted so in spite of an occasional sob from her while she worked I knew that she was aroused by her demeaning position.

While she worked she occasionally looked up at me with those sultry eyes. I knew what she wanted. Her perky breasts and taut bottom longed for my touch. I was so tempted to indulge myself in her pleasures but that was not my plan. I would deny her pleasure while I handled other more pressing matters. I would see to it that a build-up of her submissive desire would be her undoing. Once other matters were complete she would be desperate to capitulate to me willingly and then I would have it all.

That day my maid saw to the laundry, cooked my meals and otherwise waited on me. I suppose for the new Miss Chastity Belden it was her dream come true. I laughed at the irony of it all. Imagine a wealthy woman unsatisfied with her position being turned into a simple maid because her clitoris desired it? How amusing was that? I could see it in her eyes. Her lust for sex kept her hard at work in her maid uniform. For her it was like heaven.

I had a delivery that day. The driver stared lustily at the uniformed maid when she answered the door. The fact that she paid little attention to his ogling reinforced my evaluation of her. She had clear desires for a woman but no such need for a man. That was fine with me.

That evening I had her use the hair color that had been delivered by the driver to return my own blonde hair back to its natural black color. The maid worked the color in while we spoke.

"I'm to meet tomorrow with Miss Billingham. What do I need to know about her?"

"Miss Trish Anne Billingham is knowledgeable though quite prudish. She is in control of my, I mean *your* fortune, so be nice to her. Only she knows where the funds are held and releasing control of the funds is solely at her discretion."

"I see. I'll take care of her. While I rinse out my hair you are to exchange the clothes from the guest room with those gowns in my closet. In the morning I'll wear the leather catsuit. Be sure to set it out for me."

"But Miss Travers I would never…"

"Did I ask for your opinion girl?"

"No Miss Travers but…"

"That's enough for now. You are dismissed."

The maid scurried off. For sure the morning would be interesting.

That evening when she changed out the clothing in the big bedroom she took her diary with her. She moved it to the servant's quarters where she kept it in a drawer under her panties. It was no matter. I still enjoyed reading her innermost thoughts.

Today I became a domestic maid! I would have never thought that I could orgasm just from scrubbing the floor but incredibly today I did. I worked under the watchful eye of Miss Travers and it was unbelievably erotic to do so. She kept gazing at me and I tried to keep my dress enticingly situated while I was down on my hands and knees in order to tempt her. I hope that she plans on taking advantage of me because I find her to be very hot.

In the days that followed I continued to read every entry she made in it while she worked.

CHAPTER 15. Miss Trish Anne Billingham

The maid had helped me into my catsuit and I stood in front of the mirror assessing my look. With my flowing black hair I was unmistakably Miss Deanna Travers. The blonde standing next to me in her uniform was clearly my maid. I was pleased with my new presentation.

When I was ready to leave I took her purse and opened up the wallet. The picture on the driver's license was perfect. It was indisputable. I was Miss Deanna Travers.

Maid Chastity had given me all of the information that I needed. She received a small monthly allowance for expenses from accounts that held her inheritance. Miss Trish Anne Billingham administered the fortune in investment accounts that were held in her name. Miss Billingham collected a fee for her time and effort. But the catch was that she didn't know where the funds were held, only Miss Billingham knew and it was at the discretion of Miss Billingham when to give her full access to the funds.

When I arrived at the large home of Miss Billingham the look on Miss Billingham's face told me everything I needed to know about her. Clearly Chastity had misjudged the woman. She looked at me with amazement and something else that was quite familiar.

"Miss Travers, you look…different…"

I took a deep breath and glared at her with all of the power and allure that I could muster.

"Do I? Well I feel different. Things are going to be much different from now on. To start with you are going to turn my funds over to me. If you are lucky I'll continue to allow you to manage them but I will take what I want when I want."

"I see. I'm not so sure about that. My instructions are that giving you access is at my discretion and only at my discretion. You have no say in the matter."

She gave me a long look then she licked her lips.

"I suppose that I could be convinced if properly motivated to turn over whatever you desire."

I could tell by the look in her eyes what kind of motivation that she had in mind.

"Perhaps I could drop by again this evening and we could discuss it further. Would that *satisfy* you?

She smiled.

"That would be acceptable. Yes of course it would. Such things are best experienced after dark. I would think that if you come by this evening we could get right down to it and perhaps culminate in a climactic agreement. Wouldn't you say?"

Yes, I knew precisely what she wanted. I grinned back at her.

CHAPTER 16. Love Nest

It was dark when Miss Billingham opened the door to receive me. I was still in my catsuit and I carried a briefcase in with me so that I could carry paperwork back with me. I stepped inside and she greeted me with a warm embrace. It was just a hug at first but Miss Billingham didn't waste any time. Clearly she knew precisely what the price would be for the information that I needed.

She pulled me tight and our tongues entwined before I pushed her away and I tore her blouse open. There was no pretense here. It would be simple a sexual quid pro quo. I knew what she wanted and I was going to give it to her with no questions asked. Then I would have what I wanted and I would go on my way an enriched woman.

It's not like loving her was a chore. She was attractive enough to warm a girl's heart. In my mind she would be a simple pleasant evening's interlude before I returned home to my new estate with funds in hand.

She was so willing that I felt like I was taking advantage of her. Perhaps I was. Even before I peeled her clothes off in the bedroom her musky scent of sex was unmistakable. She must have longed for Miss Travers well before I came along. There was no other explanation for her lust. I was just doing what poor Miss Travers never had the initiative to attempt.

She had a king sized bed that was made for a queen. We made good use of it. I put her down on her back and then slowly undressed her. I made sure to tantalize her every step of the way while being careful not to get her too aroused. At least not too aroused at first.

Before long we were both naked and humping away at each other like we were out of control teenagers. We fucked over and over again vulva to vulva until our animal passions were satiated. I never knew that my body could reach such fervent heights. She loved me like only a woman could.

Somewhere in the evening between orgasms my body betrayed my feelings. While we whispered to each other like true lovers I realized that I was actually falling in love with Trish. There was nothing that she could ask me for that I could possibly refuse. I tried to deny it. After all she was supposed to be a conquest on my way to inherited riches but it didn't turn out that way.

Instead she had stolen my heart with an evening of ardent love making that I could never possibly forget.

She was such a beautiful lady with such a beautiful mind. She sweet talked me into letting her keep the accounts in her capable hands for safekeeping with the promise of more interludes in the future. I thought that I had finally found true love. I was naked in bed and satiated from a night of lovemaking when I agreed with her idea of safekeeping my fortune.

CHAPTER 17. Tea Party

Chastity had briefed me on the ladies group. It seemed to me like it would be a typical gathering of wealthy ladies intent on conventional socializing. I chose a black pantsuit with a matching choker collar for the occasion. I wanted to give the impression to the group that things had changed with the arrival of the new Deanna Travers.

The group wasn't all that large. Miss Danielle Stevens was the first to arrive followed by Miss Beverly Hinton, Miss Paulette Jones and Miss Georgette Broadworth. I was told that one member was missing that night since she was tending to other matters and that I would meet her at the next meeting. The last of the ladies to arrive was Miss Isabella Ellsworth.

All them appeared to be much younger than I had expected wealthy socialites to be. I was surprised by their attire too. Rather than a refined ladies tea party they seemed to look more like a group of Wall Street executives. Pantsuits were the attire of choice in black, leather and leopard skin styles.

Miss Ellsworth seemed to be the leader of the group. She was elegantly dressed in a blue pin striped designer pantsuit. With her chic shoes her outfit likely cost more than a typical house payment. She was definitely a woman of means. She struck me to be a bit of a dyke. I could see by her demeanor that she was accustomed to getting what she wanted. She took one look at maid Chastity and immediately voiced her approval.

"Why Deanna you've made changes! You've finally seen to the finer things in life—your very own maid! How domestic of you! She's such a sweet looking girl!"

She gave a lick of her lips and then she turned her attention to me.

"My how you've so suddenly grown up. Look at you—finally rid of those dreadful gowns and wearing something much more appropriate. I wholeheartedly approve! Kudos for the new look."

The ladies gathered in the sitting room while maid Chastity busied herself with tea service. I can only imagine what a come down it must have been like for her to be serving her former associates dressed in such a skimpy uniform. Every move she made immodestly flashed a bit of panty. I don't know how she managed to humiliate herself in that way. Yet Chastity did just that all while clearing dishes and filling drinks like a simple domestic maid at work.

I wondered what such sophisticated guests would think if they knew that the maid working so diligently to serve them was in fact the former Deanna Travers. Without much protest the maid had fallen from the peak of society to the trough of domestic servitude. I thought that they might laugh at the humiliation that the former Deanna Travers had brought upon herself so willingly becoming a servant in her own home at the beck and call of her own maid.

Certainly refined women don't do such things. If they also knew what a lesbian tart the maid had been in the bedroom no doubt they would administer a spanking of their own to further put her in her place.

Watching the ruse so successfully unfold made me feel absolutely brilliant. Nobody questioned anything. They accepted me as the true Miss Deanna Travers. Even better Miss Chastity Belden was believed to be my domestic maid.

The evening was mostly uneventful. The ladies chatted over this investment deal and that opportunity without much more of general interest to me. I found myself somewhat out of place with no business of my own to offer the group. I couldn't very well brag of my greatest accomplishment—stealing the life and wealth from my former employer.

The ladies did comment on Chastity. Apparently they were impressed with her abilities. They noted how cute her outfit was and how accomplished a server that she was. I felt like I had made a good call putting the former Miss Travers into her new role.

Naturally they inquired as to how I came upon her. I guess good help is hard to find. All of them commented how they wished that they knew where to find such a talented maid. I told them that she just showed up at my front door one morning and that I was impressed with her willingness to work.

In particular I couldn't help but notice Miss Ellsworth taking repeated glances at Chastity. She tried to be unobtrusive but I was on to her. Her longing looks gave away her desires. It was precisely the opening that I was looking for.

The guests systematically left the party until only Miss Ellsworth remained. She was in no hurry to go perhaps, I thought, because she was enjoying the view and attentions of my alluring maid. It was only then that I made my move.

"Miss Ellsworth…"

"Sweetie why be so formal? Please call me Isabella."

"Isabella I do have business to conduct."

"Please do dear."

"You hold the deed to my mansion in your possession. I wonder how I might go about retrieving it."

"Oh? I must say I thought that you would never ask. What took you so long?"

I glanced over at Chastity. She stood in the background with her head lowered. Clearly she had simply been too shy to make an inquiry.

"Had I known a request would suffice I would have asked earlier. If that was all that was necessary then would you please see fit to simply turn it over to me?"

She gave me a mischievous devilish grin.

"Of course not. Why would I do that?"

I should have known it wouldn't be so easy.

"Perhaps I can entice you. You are a sophisticated woman who would seem to have everything. What may I ask would you care to have from me?"

She gazed at me for a moment. Then she took a playful glance at Chastity.

"To be honest I've always fancied bedding you. I even thought about taking you by force but you seemed so untouched. I felt that you were far too innocent for such wickedness on my part. I imagined that one day you would mature and that you would ask me for the deed. My plan was to exchange your deed for a playful frolic in my brass bed. Look at you! That day has come. But I've changed my mind about that."

"Oh?"

"Yes. I think I have other interests.

"Do tell."

"Your maid. What is her name?"

70

"My maid?"

"Yes the maid."

"Her name is Chastity Belden—a charming flower if ever there was one. She is rather shy though and not very proficient in matters of the bedroom. She is practically a virgin."

She laughed.

"Practically a virgin you say? A girl is either a virgin or she isn't. Which is it?"

"She is not what I would call worldly by any means. She was quite pure until I had my way with her. I've bedded her only once."

"I like to say that first-hand knowledge is always best in such matters. So she is not a virgin but she is certainly an untrained novice. You say that you have bedded her? Okay. That is splendid. So we know that she is…of our refined persuasion then?"

"Yes of course she is. She is *so* into women and she relishes the touch of a strong woman. She is a bit odd though. She has a deep-seated desire to be dominated in the bedroom. She has a strong yearning to be paddled on her bare behind. So I don't think that I would coddle the girl though we did do a bit of spooning."

Rather than dissuade Isabella that only seemed to offer her further encouragement.

"A shy young girl who likes to be dominated! Plus she is in need of training and experience! Perfect! I couldn't have asked for anything more. Of course I wouldn't want to have her unless she were agreeable."

I thought a bit of a gamble was in order. I motioned to Chastity who had been listening carefully to our conversation.

"Come here girl."

The maid stood next to us at attention.

"Lift your dress girl and lower your panties so that Miss Ellsworth may test your level of excitement."

It was a challenging moment for Chastity. She clearly fought the urge to humiliate herself in the presence of Isabella. She likely had thought of herself as equals with the woman until this gathering. For her this would be the final degradation that would seal her lowly position as a humble domestic maid. Only a lowly obedient servant would debase herself in such a manner. However she seemingly knew her place and the excitement of the moment got the better of her.

Rather than to disobey her new Mistress she capitulated. You might say that her own love of self-degradation won the day and with blushing face she lifted her dress and lowered her panties for Isabella to brazenly inspect the condition of her genitals.

If Chastity received sexual gratification from the order it was Isabella who was astonished by her level of obedience and who was most amused. She gave a slight giggle before she fingered Chastity's wetness and then teased at her clitoris with a caress of her fingers. Chastity moaned in erotic pleasure at the gentle caress.

"My, my, Deanna your maid is sopping wet at the mere idea of serving me. I should say that she agrees wholeheartedly with a possible bargain."

She looked the maid straight in the eyes.

"You do enjoy this don't you maid Chastity? You are nothing but a shy maid in need of a dominant woman to fulfill your needs. I should think that I could do that for you both day and night."

The maid stayed at attention with her head down holding her dress up with her shaved sex fully exposed while we discussed the terms of her surrender.

"If I were to lend her to you what would become of her?"

"Oh I would think the usual. I would take her over my knee and spank her like an errant child. Then I believe that I could make her purr with desire like an obedient kitten. I would tease her unmercifully until she could no longer resist my attentions. Then I would make her beg for satisfaction.

After that I can I imagine our bodies pressing together pelvis to pelvis humping away in a most heated fashion. Yes, I would introduce her to the heights that only another woman can provide her with. Afterwards I would take out my strapon and fuck out whatever else was left of her brains."

"Both front and back?"

"Of course."

"And then she would be returned to me?"

"I would have to introduce her to a double dildo first. Such a lovely flower should be acquainted with all manner of sexual capitulation. Only then would I consider returning her to you. She would be a complete fully fucked submissive trained and ready to do the bidding of any woman so inclined who came her way."

It was precisely what I wanted to hear.

"This could all be accomplished in say one week in exchange for my deed?"

"Oh for goodness sake no. One week would never do, not for such a playful time. I should think six weeks at a minimum would suffice."

It seemed like a long time to go without domestic service. I was after all getting used to Chastity doing all of the chores. I was however in the mood to bargain with her like she was a precious commodity.

I took a look at Chastity. There was no hiding her desire. She was so excited! Clearly she approved of such a tawdry agreement. Her breathing was heavy and her face was still flushed a deep red. Her sex shamefully glistened with moisture.

"Four weeks. You may have her for four weeks in exchange for the deed."

Isabella laughed.

"Is your maid worth so much to you that you would haggle over her wares? She must be special. I look forward to making her my personal harlot. Five weeks and that's my final offer."

"Done!"

She smiled in triumph before she continued.

"One more thing dear. You wouldn't let me leave here without at least tasting your pleasure. I need to satisfy my curiosity. Let's kiss to seal the deal."

She turned to me, cupped my buttocks with firm hands and then her mouth eagerly covered mine. Her tongue slithered inside of me in a passionate embrace of eager serpents. I couldn't help myself. I gave a whimper of agreeable pleasure while her hands shifted position and she explored my breasts with a soft gentle tease. Finally she backed away.

"Every bit as tasty as I thought you would be. You respond well to my temptations. I sense that you are submissive yourself. Perhaps once I've had my way with your maid I'll return and bargain for *your* goods. I do believe that you have deceived me all of this time. I can tell that you would be very agreeable to a similar arrangement. You would make a fine lover and perhaps an even better maid."

My mouth stayed open but no words came out. Her words had touched something deep inside of me that I thought best not to reveal. I feared that I gave it away when I found that I could not meet her gaze. I lowered my eyes in an attempt to hide my feelings. She seemed to realize what she had done. She gave a little knowing laugh.

"I'll send an Uber over in the morning to transport the maid. There's a team of two girls that we've used before. They do a fine job with this kind of delivery. They're very discreet. Have a nice evening dear."

With that Isabella went out the door leaving us alone. She had said that *we've* used them before. I wondered what she meant by that.

CHAPTER 18. Drivers

The two young female drivers arrived promptly the first thing the next morning. They pulled up in a black paneled van. The ladies were both dressed like proper chauffeurs complete with a tiny black cap. The two women with long flowing flaming red hair appeared to be identical twins.

Though quite shapely and stunningly attractive these were not petite women. The ladies were tall in stature and quite imposing to the point of being intimidating. I hesitate to call a woman brawny but they were both quite muscular and best described to be Amazonian. They were clearly powerful women quite capable of handling any heavy package or difficult situation with no trouble at all. They came into the house with one of them carrying— clearly with ease— a large heavy suitcase that she carefully set down on the marble foyer tile with a hefty thump.

Chastity had let the drivers in but I was also standing right there to greet the girls. One of them spoke to me while ignoring the maid.

"Good morning Miss Travers. We're here to properly prepare maid Chastity for transport and to deliver her promptly to Miss Ellsworth. We were told that you are expecting us and that we are to treat her with utmost care."

I pointed to the maid.

"She's all yours."

She gave a smile.

"Very well."

I was impressed with her presentation. The girl seemed so professional. She had spoken to me very courteously. I wasn't at all prepared for what transpired next. She reached down and opened up the big suitcase revealing a full array of bondage devices. She carefully selected a leather penis gag before going behind Chastity. Then she instructed the maid to open her mouth before she inserted the phallic gag and strapped it into place. Chastity responded not with resistance but with a soft muffled whimper of aroused approval.

The two ladies worked quickly and quietly. Next came a black leather blindfold while the other driver added a leather posture collar that kept the maid's head pointed up. Then the maid stood seemingly paralyzed with lust while the driver unzipped her dress and spread it from her shoulders. The uniform dropped to the floor leaving her standing in her lingerie.

The drivers seemed oblivious to how intimately personally they were treating their package. I watched in amazement while they nonchalantly stripped Chastity naked without so much as a passing comment. They acted like they commonly prepared women for transportation in a similar manner and that it was just another day of chauffeuring for them.

Once she was relieved of her clothing they added bondage cuffs to the maid at her wrists and ankles. Then the wrist cuffs were attached to the posture collar holding Chastity's hands up by her neck.

At that point one of the drivers took the liberty of softly fingering the maid's nipples which were already lewdly firm and pointed out in a most obscene manner. There was a muffled moan beneath the penis gag that intensified when the driver found her way between Chastity's legs to a tender flicker of a touch of her clitoris.

The suitcase still held bondage surprises. A strapless bra with metal cups was placed around the maid's breasts. A medieval looking chastity belt with a vaginal phallus and a butt plug was lubed up and inserted tightly into position.

The two ankle cuffs were attached together by chain before the driver finished up by fastening a leash to the front of the posture collar. Chastity was writhing in pleasure but of course her private areas were secured from any other form of stimulation. She was left in a bondage state of tease and denial that she couldn't escape.

Finally one of the ladies reached into the suitcase and pulled out a long cape. They draped the cape over the maid's shoulders and snapped it in place covering up her indecent appearance all the way down to her ankles.

With that they were ready to leave. It occurred to me that they were supposed to give me something.

"Wait, did Miss Ellsworth say anything about a deed?"

"Oh, we almost forgot."

The driver pulled an envelope out of the suitcase.

"Miss Ellsworth instructed me to present this to you Miss Travers with her compliments."

I smiled and took the envelope from the driver. With that the driver gave a tug on the leash leading Chastity out the front door while the other driver followed behind. I watched them put the maid into the back of the van, close the door and drive off.

I quickly opened the envelope to check on my good fortune. However instead of finding a deed there was a handwritten note from Isabella.

Were you expecting your deed Miss Travers? I think not! Your kiss tells me that we have more pleasurable business to conduct. We will discuss further upon completion of satisfactory performance of my new maid.

I smiled. She was good. Isabella was very good. Such a tease! I would have to be more careful with her in the future.

CHAPTER 19. Maid Returns

The weeks went by quickly. During that time I had explored the mansion from top to bottom. The place was extensive and certainly fit for a queen. Aside from her obvious bedroom needs I could see why the former Mistress had required a maid. The place was excessively large to the point of being absurd for a single woman to live in it. I suppose that was the best part. If I chose to stay there I would need the use of my maid in more ways than one.

Eight weeks had passed since Chastity had been taken away. Isabella had called to say she wasn't ready to relinquish her until this particular morning. It was of no matter to me. I had graciously granted her an extension on our previous agreement.

The black van arrived right on schedule. I was curious how Chastity had been treated so when the van pulled up in the circular drive I peeked out through my office window to get a glimpse of her.

Only the two female chauffeurs got out of the van. Chastity was nowhere to be seen so I was a bit concerned for her welfare. The two ladies entered my home, with one of them bringing along a suitcase. They stood in the large foyer.

"Your presence is requested. Miss Ellsworth has sent us to transport you to her home."

"You must be mistaken. I understood that maid Chastity was to be returned to me today."

They seemed puzzled. They looked at each other before speaking to me again.

"Miss Ellsworth gave us no such instructions Miss Travers. We were told to transport *you*. I must warn you that those were my instructions whether you are willing or not."

"You'll do no such thing!"

"Very well Miss Travers."

I couldn't believe it. How dare Miss Ellsworth break our bargain! I want to make it quite clear that I made every effort to resist those two women. I certainly didn't come willingly. But the two women were every bit as formidable as they appeared to be.

One of them held my wrists behind me while the other blindfolded me. I wildly squirmed and frantically wiggled in a vain attempt to escape while they unzipped my dress and it fell to the floor. I tried to scream but that resulted in a penis gag being inserted into my mouth. They peeled off my lingerie and I was naked. They took my shoes off and with that my feet were bare. I tried to kick one of them but she went behind me and my wrists were cuffed and attached to a posture collar. I tried to twist away in a final valiant attempt to escape but it was useless.

By then I was already worn down from the struggle. The two laughed at my feeble effort to break away from their powerful grip. With my ankles held together with a short length of chain attached to ankle cuffs one of them stroked my vulva before inserting a finger and circling my clitoris with her thumb.

I was ashamed at my response to such a blatant assault. I knew that she would find me moistened with lust. I confirmed her suspicion with a lusty moan that surprised even me. Again they laughed at what they had done to me.

I could only stand there when they attached the metal brassiere over my breasts. I moaned in pleasure when they lubricated me front and back before securing the metal chastity belt chastity belt complete with a vaginal phallus and a butt plug tightly over my love nest. I was aroused by the treatment and totally at their mercy. I was no longer able to resist whatever Miss Ellsworth had planned for me.

I felt a cape being draped over my shoulders and snapped into place. I felt a leash tug at my neck so I took only the tiny steps the chain between my ankles allowed me to take—no doubt out the door and over to the van. I felt strong arms lift me and set me down on the floor in the back of the vehicle.

The van seemed to drive forever until it finally came to a stop and I was taken out. I felt the cool air on my face as I was slowly led away by the leash like I was some kind of obedient puppy.

CHAPTER 20. Tea Party II

I could hear ladies talking in vaguely familiar voices. They were nearby but I couldn't tell how close they were. There was raucous laughing and giggling but I couldn't make out exactly what they were laughing at. They seemed to be oblivious of me and my condition. All I could do was stand there barefoot and await my fate.

Finally there was a tug on my leash and the voices grew closer. Then there was more giggling that sounded like it came from very close by. A hand lifted the blindfold from my eyes. My head was pointed upward from the posture collar so while my eyes adjusted to the light I strained my eyes to peer downward. Slowly a group of ladies came into view.

They were all staring at me. It was the whole ladies tea party group led by Miss Isabella Ellsworth. To my surprise Miss Trish Anne Billingham was also casually sitting with the group.

Chastity was standing next to Miss Ellsworth dressed in a plain maid serving uniform. She had her gaze lowered in a subservient position. I could see that she wore a leather collar around her neck that had SLUT spelled out in bold rhinestone letters.

Miss Ellsworth spoke first.

"I see Deanna that you've met our distinguished drivers Lonnie and Donnie. They seem to have made you quite comfortable."

The group chuckled at my situation.

"Forgive me dear. Perhaps introductions are in order. Ladies, please meet the *real* Miss Chastity Belden. She attempted to take advantage of Miss Deanna Travers and her submissive personality in order to gain her fortune. Thankfully my new maid was kind enough to share her story with me."

I couldn't believe it. Deanna had sold me out!

"Maid Deanna show us your Sapphic Promise. Please display yourself for Miss Belden."

It had to be so humiliating for the maid but nevertheless she hardly hesitated. She immediately lifted her dress and the plain white slip that was beneath it. She wasn't wearing panties. Her shaved genitals were clearly visible framed nicely by her white garter belt and the tabs holding up her stockings.

Surrounding her clitoris was a golden clit clip with tiny golden jewelry chains that dangled down over her hairless vulva. I could see that every movement of her body would cause the strands of chain to gently tease her.

I had a quick glimpse of her eyes before she lowered her gaze again. She didn't seem to be in distress. I had seen that look on her before. She had the most lovely bedroom eyes. She was obviously highly aroused and was clearly enjoying the blissful sensations being provided by the golden chains. She was seemingly in a far-off world of tantalizing pleasures somewhat oblivious to my presence. Miss Ellsworth continued.

"My dear Miss Belden this leaves you with quite the dilemma. As you see Miss Travers is wearing a clit clip as a sign of total surrender of her body to me. She has such a pretty clitty doesn't she? She does my bidding both in and out of my bedroom. She is now my submissive maid servant.

I believe that you have the same submissive qualities as Miss Travers. You may surrender your body as well or I can turn you over to the police. It is your choice. I can assure you that if you resist Miss Travers will press charges and that you will spend the rest of your life in jail tending to the sexual needs of other female prisoners. What will it be?"

I tried to speak in vehement protest but the penis gag prevented anything other than a muffled murmur of a sound. The ladies laughed before Miss Ellsworth continued.

"We'll take that to be a yes. I've arranged a little amusement here for your benefit. Ladies please give me your sealed bids."

The ladies each gave a white envelope to Miss Ellsworth. Then Miss Ellsworth began to open them one at a time.

"Miss Belden you should know that you are in high demand. The first two bids are quite substantial. Miss Jones is out of the running and right now you stand to be the property of Miss Hinton."

She opened another envelope.

"Oh Georgette you bested Miss Hinton and you are in the lead!"

She opened another envelope.

"Sorry Danielle, you didn't make the cut."

The final envelope belonged to Miss Billingham. As shameful as it was to be sold at auction I found myself hoping that I would be hers. If I had to become a servant then I wanted to serve the attractive Miss Billingham. Then I caught myself. I didn't want to become a servant like Deanna had become! She looked to be so humiliated! Even while the envelopes were being opened she still held her dress up for everyone to see her privates. Apparently she didn't dare lower her dress without being instructed to do so.

"Congratulations Trish you are now the proud owner of maid Chastity."

The ladies all applauded the winner. Isabella handed a golden key to Trish which I presumed went to my chastity belt. Trish motioned and one of the Amazon girls came forward. Trish handed her the key.

"Take her to my estate and prepare her properly. Make her a blonde and style that hair into something more suitable for a working maid.

Long hair like that will only get in the way in my bedroom so there is no point to it. I'll be home in a few hours to take possession of the girl."

"Yes Miss Billingham."

With that my blindfold was put back in place and the ladies went out of view.

CHAPTER 21. A Good Girl

The drive seemed to take forever. I could tell by the bumpy ride that a gravel road was involved and I was quite rattled by the time the van finally came to a halt. The trip gave me time to consider my plight. I decided that it was best to cooperate until I had a reasonable chance to escape. Then I changed my mind. I didn't want to go to jail. I really didn't know what to do.

I was lifted out of the van. I felt the tug of the leash so I took tiny little steps in the direction that I was led. I felt cement turn to smooth tile underneath my bare feet. I could hear Donnie and Lonnie chatting away while they led me along until I heard a door open. I was led forward and then I heard the door close.

My blindfold was removed. I was standing in front of a vanity and I could see the reflection of Donnie and Lonnie standing behind me. One of them put a hand on my shoulder and pressured me down onto a chair.

I sat motionless watching in the mirror while the girls decided who would be my stylist. They both wanted a chance to "Make the bitch look like a servant". Eventually I heard "Okay you win. Donnie you do the honors" before Donnie picked up scissors from the vanity.

I wanted to beg them for mercy but the penis restraint that gagged me prohibited any words. I thought that if I could only reason with them maybe they would let me go or at least spare my lovely hair that took months to grow. Instead in just a few minutes my beautiful long black hair was reduced to plain short bob similar to the style that I had reduced Deanna to just a few weeks earlier.

Then I watched in horror while Lonnie opened a package of hair color and worked it into what little was left of my diminished head of hair. If that wasn't bad enough Lonnie decided to taunt me while she worked the product in.

"You'll make such a pretty little maid for Miss Billingham. I'll bet you're so excited to get started. I'm sure that you have much to offer in the bedroom. I'd take you myself but we're not allowed to do that. At least not yet. Would you protest very much if we decided to fuck with you?"

I tried to answer that I most certainly would protest but of course unintelligible garble came out. The ladies laughed. Lonnie continued.

"I think she wants us to fuck her. She is such a horny little slut! Donnie get the enema bag. We'll do her while the color sets."

All I could think of was *anything* but that. But Donnie left and quickly returned rolling a cart that had an enema bag hanging from it that was teeming with fluid. Who keeps such a thing in the household? That thought alone was frightening. I watched in the mirror while Donnie removed my cape and I was yanked to my feet. Then Lonnie used the golden key to remove my chastity belt. In the process she stroked my vulva with a soft caress of her hand in a manner that only a woman could provide.

"Donnie she's sopping wet! What a slut. She is such a fucking whore. Do you think that Miss Billingham will let us play with her?"

"She let us play with the last one so why not with this one too? We'll get to fuck her brains out later. By the time we're done with her she'll be a blonde ditz brain just like the last one."

The last one? How many girls had these women abducted? I wasn't about to let them fuck my brains out that's for sure. It would take more than two Amazon women to turn my brain to mush. Even if they were dominant and rather attractive I would never become a ditz brain.

I wanted so much to resist them. But then Donnie touched my clit and I closed my eyes and gave an unintended moan of pleasure. I felt two hands on my body and just like that I was over the lap of one of the Amazon girls with my butt up in the air. Again I tried to protest but it was useless. It was futile for me to struggle against their strength. The ladies were far too powerful for me to resist them.

I felt rubber fingers applying a greasy lubricant in a place that those fingers shouldn't have been in. Then the nozzle went where the fingers had just probed. I recognized Lonnie's voice and I realized that it was her lap that I was bent over.

"There, there little slut. Soon you'll feel all nice and full and before you know it you'll be ready for Miss Billingham to take you front and back to places you've never been before."

The fluid slowly drained into my bottom swelling me up inside giving me a very uncomfortable warm sensation.

When the enema bag finally drained itself I was pulled up off of Lonnie's lap. I stood there with the tube still in my bottom holding the fluid in place while Donnie positioned herself in front of me. Lonnie started taking the cuffs off my ankles while she spoke.

"Listen to me slut. We're going to get you naked and then we're going to take you to your room so you can expel your enema and then we'll bathe you. When we finish with you you'll stay there like a good girl until Miss Ellsworth comes for you. If you give us trouble then Donnie is going to spank you like a naughty school girl and you won't be able to sit for a week. Do you understand me?"

All I could do was nod my head and grunt in agreement. After the enema treatment I knew that they meant what they were saying so I didn't dare risk a spanking. They removed the cuffs and the metal bra leaving me with just the penis gag and the collar with the leash attached. Then with the enema nozzle still in place they walked me down a hallway by the leash with the enema cart in tow until we came to a small room.

It turned out to be the servant's quarters. Compressed into the tiny dreary room was a single bed, a nightstand, a dresser with a mirror, a closet and an attached bathroom just big enough for a toilet and a tub. There was a lone window that revealed it was still dark outside. They removed the nozzle and I sat on the toilet and expelled the enema while they ran bubbly soapy water in the tub.

CHAPTER 22. Miss Billingham Claims Her Prize

The bath left me scented with a flowery fragrance that seemed to fill the room. I wasn't sure what was worse. Was it the groping that Lonnie had done while I was in the tub or was it the position I found myself in afterwards?

Lonnie had taken great pleasure in personally making sure every inch of my body was scrubbed clean while I was in the tub. Her fingers had flittered over my erect nipples and then probed inside my vagina while Donnie had looked on with glee. I had been teased to the point of no return when Lonnie ordered me out of the tub and into a towel that Donnie used to casually dry every inch of my body.

Then they took me out to the bed and chained me tightly spread-eagle to it. With my collar removed and my penis gag removed I was left alone naked to contemplate my fate. I had no idea how long I had waited in that position or what time it was when I heard the door open and Miss Billingham came into the room.

She was in no hurry to take her pleasure of me. Instead she down sat on the bed.

"Chastity I know that you are a submissive girl and that you most certainly are enjoying yourself today. You had best not deny that. I will not keep you here against your will. In fact your own lust will keep you here as my willing servant. You will be my house maid and my willing whore."

She placed a clit clip similar to the one that Deanna had been wearing on the nightstand.

"After I'm through with you tonight I will leave the door unlocked so the decision is yours. This is your Sapphic Promise. I expect you to wear it in the morning along with the maid uniform that is in the closet. Doing so is your acceptance that you will serve me like a common maid. You will not be offered any clothing other than what you will find in this room. Your sex will always be available to whoever I decide so you'll find no panties here. If you wear the Sapphic Promise you are giving your clit to me and you will not touch yourself there unless ordered by me to do so.

You should realize that this mansion is surrounded by woods miles very much secluded from civilization down a dirt road. If you decide to leave you should follow the road otherwise you may get lost in the woods.

 I'm going to release you soon. Like I said the door will not be locked and you will be free to go. But I hope that the pleasures that you will find here are strings that will keep you here and hold you in servitude."

She stroked my gorged clitoris and I closed my eyes. Just as I arched upward to meet her touch she stopped her tease.

"Tonight you will service me. If you perform suitably you'll be allowed to do the same tomorrow."

I could feel her removing the chains that held me in place. She positioned herself next to me on her back waiting to be lovingly undressed. I had been teased for so long that it didn't take any more encouragement than that for me to begin to strip her. My hands shook while I peeled off layers of her clothing until she lay before me naked on the bed.

I smothered her nude body in soft seductive kisses that teased and tantalized her lust. She breathed heavily while she squirmed and writhed in pleasure. My tongue touched her nipples and my fingers tickled her clitoris while she bucked and moaned in pleasure to my touch.

Ultimately my tongue licked its way to her inner thighs and then to her shaved vulva. Her back arched while my tongue toyed with her engorged clitoris.

Finally her body shook with a climatic orgasm and she screamed out in lustful pleasure to my ministrations. Her pussy gushed its appreciation while I pressed my lips to her sex and I worshipped her honey pot. She was gasping for breath when I finally stretched out next to her and we cuddled together the way two lovers should.

Miss Billingham was nowhere near finished playing. After a few moments she sat up and took a strapon from under the bed. Upon fitting it securely on herself she turned me over on my stomach and fucked me like I was a common whore from behind.

Pegged by the long dong of the strapon I had no choice but to helplessly ride along, my face pushed into the pillow with my tits swinging freely while she pumped into me until I screamed in orgasmic pleasure and then hung limp in her embrace. Afterwards she turned me over on the bed so that I faced her.

Then she removed the faux penis from the strapon and held it to my mouth. I am ashamed to say that at her urging while she stroked my shortened hair I then licked it and sucked it clean.

For the final indignity she turned me back over and used the strapon on me again—this time on my rear end. I suppose that she wanted to show me that she could take me any way that she wanted. By that point I simply purred like a kitten while she plunged deep into me with abandon.

After that she left me alone on my bed and I immediately fell asleep.

I found myself delirious with delightful bliss. I had been transported to a whole new level of erotic pleasure and I didn't want it to ever end. Miss Billingham was everything I ever wanted in a lover and much more. I began to realize that I would never be able to leave her because I could never possibly find another woman who could make love to me like she could.

CHAPTER 23. Maid Chastity

The light shining from the window woke me. It couldn't have been more than an hour or two since Miss Billingham had her way with me. Her musky scent still filled my nostrils and delighted my senses. I staggered to the bathroom and ran water over my face. When I emerged my eye went to the nightstand and the Sapphic Promise clit clip that was still waiting there.

I knew that I could walk out the door that very instant. Still the magic lure of the clit clip beckoned. Would it hurt to look around and see what else was in the room to wear? I decided it would not.

I opened a drawer. True to Miss Billingham's word there were no panties. Just plain white cotton brassieres, plain white garter belts, and heavy duty taupe stockings. There was nothing fancy there. They were the undergarments of a plain working maid.

I felt a shiver and my nipples hardened. I decided to clip a bra on if only for comfort. A garter belt followed and I smoothed on stockings. Just for warmth, of course.

I wondered what was in the closet. If I was to make a mad dash for freedom I couldn't very well do it in lingerie could I? The closet contained simple full white slips that hung next to rather plain maid uniforms each with a half apron carefully wrapped around it. They were the kind of uniform that you might find on a hotel maid. On the floor were black patent leather heels. On the shelf above were white mob caps. I wondered how the uniform would look on me. Of course I had to try on at least one of the uniforms just to see.

There were more trembles of pure pleasure when I finally tied the apron on. How could such humiliation excite me like that? I had no idea.

When I looked in the mirror I saw a reflection of the same woman that Deanna had appeared to be. It sent an approving tingle of satisfaction through my body that twitched deep inside of me and that ended at the tip of my rosebud. I didn't expect that kind of feeling at all but I couldn't deny that it was there.

I was a plain blonde maid with my hair cut into a practical bob that only a working girl would wear. I was dressed for work, not play, certainly very subservient appearing. It was certainly not the sexy attire of a French maid. Instead clearly it was the attire of a true domestic servant.

My eye went to the nightstand. I wondered—what did it feel like to wear a clit clip? There was only one way to find out—who would know? I carefully slid it into position. I held my dress up and looked in the mirror at the submissive girl who had made the Sapphic Promise. The little tiny chains flittered like tiny little feathers at my vulva. The sensation was erotic and far too tempting to pass up. I took a deep breath. Would it really hurt to see what Miss Billingham had in mind for me?

I gazed at the servant girl in the mirror and the look in her eyes easily answered my question. The night before had been so lovely. She had to feel what it was like to serve such an authoritative woman. The girl in the mirror knew best.

The new maid was ready for work. I smoothed my dress down and slowly walked out the door of my room.

CHAPTER 24. Lonnie and Donnie

To my surprise the two Amazon ladies were waiting for me in the hallway. I soon discovered that the two girls were far more than just drivers.

The two ladies had been stationed outside my room either to escort me outside or to familiarize me with my duties. They were the enforcers of the tea party clutch and were not at all afraid to enforce the rules of the house upon any submissive who came their way. In this case, that would be me.

There are three types of women. There are dominant women who enjoy the pleasures of submissive women. There are submissive women who enjoy being dominated. Then there are sadistic women who take merciless pleasure in dominating and tantalizing submissive women like me. In this case that would be Lonnie and Donnie.

When they saw my attire they both giggled with delight. Donnie was the first to comment.

"Hey Lonnie look what we have here — a new maid ready and willing to be trained on behalf of

Miss Billingham. She must have enjoyed her little frolic last night."

Donnie gave a fiendish grin. I made no effort to resist when she lifted my dress and my slip to see if I had made the Sapphic promise. She was pleased with what she saw.

"I told you. I knew she couldn't resist. We're going to have loads of fucking fun with this one."

She let go of my dress and turned to Lonnie. Lonnie immediately produced a leather collar that she secured tightly around my neck. It was very familiar. It was identical to the collar that I had seen Deanna wearing the night before. Somehow I felt even more obedient to the whim of the two ladies once I was wearing a leather collar around my neck that had SLUT spelled out in bold rhinestone letters. Donnie was explicit with her instructions.

"You'll wear the collar at all times. You are not to appear without it or there will be consequences. The collar is your reminder that you are a slut and a slave. You will not speak unless spoken to and if spoken to you will respond with respect. Address me with Miss Lonnie and address my associate with Miss Donnie. Naturally you will also address Miss Billingham accordingly. Do you understand girl?"

"Yes Miss Lonnie."

I felt another tingle of arousal. I had never before realized that I was so submissive and what a thrill it was to me. The tiny chains were doing their deed playfully dancing over my pubes. I wanted to moan with pleasure. What would the ladies do to me if I gave a swoon of delight?

I wouldn't find out. They immediately put me to work washing the kitchen floor. Donnie and Lonnie chatted merrily away while carefully watching me down on all fours polishing the ceramic tile.

I learned that Miss Trish Anne Billingham would take no part in training me. That was the job of the two sadistic women. They were strict, authoritative no nonsense sadists. I found that out the hard way when I complained hours later about needing a break from my chores.

I had broken an important rule. I had spoken out of turn.

CHAPTER 25. Put To The Dildo

I would find out much later that the twins were instructed by Miss Billingham not to have sex with me. In fact they were not even supposed to touch me. Miss Billingham had forbidden it. They were expected to strictly supervise me while meticulously training me to be Miss Billingham's housemaid. However there was a very important catch. She had told them that if I disobeyed them, or if I needed discipline for sloppy work or if I otherwise became a problem for them they were free to do with me whatever they pleased. It was actually a cruel license for the twins to have their way with me because they saw to it that there was always an exception to the rule. In retrospect I suppose that Miss Billingham wanted it that way.

If ever there were true Amazon women who reveled in taking pleasure of another woman they were Lonnie and Donnie. They reveled in the joy of my mistakes so that they would be free to use me however they desired. That meant that they could indulge themselves with my sexual offerings at will with even the slightest infraction of rules or with less than perfect work. By being absurdly strict authoritarian supervisors they made sure that there were plenty of occasions for them to take advantage of the situation.

They had a sadistic side that seemed to give them satisfaction at every opportunity. They enjoyed teasing me, applying the paddle to my bottom, putting me in bondage and otherwise playing humiliating games that would usually leave me denied of carnal gratification and panting for more.

I never knew for sure which game I would be subjected to. At times they would tease and deny me until I begged them to bring me to orgasm. Then they would laugh at me and leave me exhausted but unfulfilled. Other times they would force me to climax multiple times until I was fully spent and unable to muster the energy to even move. In both cases when they were done playing their games I would be put in strict bondage to contemplate their supreme superiority.

I learned everything that I needed to know about the twins that first time I spoke out of turn. Donnie and Lonnie took turns walloping me over their knees while I begged and pleaded for mercy that never came. I lay crying and completely exhausted from the struggle over Lonnie's lap before the assault stopped and I was allowed to stand up.

With my bottom burning and stinging form the punishment I was led to a bedroom. While I fought and struggled the ladies stripped me naked. Exhausted from the struggle all I could do was stand helplessly and watch them while they hungrily eyed my nude body. Donnie saw fit to laugh at my situation.

"Did we mention honey that your punishment wasn't over yet?"

Lonnie made herself comfortable on the bed and Donnie pushed me down between Lonnie's legs. My bottom still stung from the paddling. I was held there between Lonnie's powerful legs with my face pushed up against her sex. I couldn't help but take in the sweet fragrance of her excitement. Donnie gave me orders. She told me that my punishment for improper use of my tongue was to lap at her musky sex until she shrieked and screamed in not one but two voluptuous Amazonian orgasms.

While I lapped away at Lonnie Donnie removed my clit clip and then mounted me from behind using a strapon to penetrate me. My body was too weak to resist her and with her constant thrusting my body eventually betrayed me and moved in time to her lusty rhythm.

I synchronized the tempo of my tongue with each pulse of the strapon. So Donnie used her hips to control the pleasure that I transmitted straight to Lonnie. Eventually Lonnie submitted to the attention I gave to her clitoris with not one but two lusty orgasms just like I had been ordered to pleasure her with.

By the time Lonnie relaxed her legs and released her grip on me I felt like a limp ragdoll. But the twins weren't done just yet. They exchanged positions and I was forced to lap at Donnie's cunt like I was a hungry kitten at the urging of the corresponding thrust of Lonnie's strapon. When Donnie finally came for the second time I collapsed from fatigue unable to even muster the energy to move from the bed.

The ladies laughed at my predicament. They hardly seemed at all spent by the effort. It was more like they had been invigorated by the erotic romp. Sadistic right to the end, Lonnie procured rope from somewhere and in just a few moments I was hogtied on the bed unable to so much as twitch a muscle. Donnie stuck a dildo gag into my mouth and after she tightened it firmly into position I was blindfolded.

I was far too drained to make any attempt to escape. My helpless used up body could only hold the position hogtied on my stomach so I was resigned to complete surrender until the twins saw fit to release me.

They left me bound up like that for the rest of the day with only the itching of my chafed vagina and the burning sensation on my buttocks to keep me company.

It would be hours before Donnie and Lonnie returned and playfully set me free. Even then I was so stiff that from the bondage that the two of them had to take me by the arms and lead me to my quarters. After a final slap on my bottom I was deposited on my bed and left for the night.

That first time I learned never to talk back to them ever again. But still that was not the end of their total domination of me. On other occasions I found myself tied naked to a wooden chair helplessly staring at myself in the mirror.

While that might not sound so bad sitting for a long period with a sore bottom on the wooden chair was not very pleasant. Having my tongue in an O-ring gag didn't help much either. With my hands tied behind me and with my legs tied spread apart to the legs of the chair I was held wide open for teasing. Donnie in particular seemed to enjoy posing me like that.

The ladies shared a bedroom that featured an expansive wooden four poster bed. One evening in one of their crueler punishments they tied me to a post at the foot of the bed. Blindfolded, gagged and with my clit clip in place I was unable to move a muscle. I could only listen to their lewd lovemaking that took places inches away.

The sounds of their passion awoke my own feelings. With my nipples fully erect and my juices flowing onto the bed my muffled passionate pleas to join them was met with giggles and laughter. Even though I couldn't see them I knew what they were doing. Continual shrieks of pleasure and the sounds of licking and kissing meant that they were enjoying multiple orgasms that no doubt were heightened for them by my sadistic humiliation. My presence only served to enhance what sounded like their ardent tribbing while at the same time their lovemaking intensified my own sexual frustration.

After their fervent evening of Lesbian lovemaking they slept in peaceful bliss while I stayed wide awake dripping yearning juices in tantalizing frustration. Both unable to satisfy myself and unable to be satisfied I would spend the endless night held in unfulfilled arousal unable to do a thing about it. The next morning I would be exhausted from a sleepless night but still expected to don a uniform and see to my chores.

There seemed to be no end to the sexual humiliation that the twins dispensed. The twins were far too physically superior for me to do anything about their enforced sex play. My own submissive tendencies kept me from making much of an effort to resist them. So I was a participant in their sex games partly because I was absolutely unable to stop them and partly because deep down I enjoyed them.

When I began to look forward to their sensual games I realized what they were doing to me. Their prediction was beginning to come true. All I could think of was having sex and having intense lusty orgasms. They were systematically fucking my brains out and I was turning into a blonde ditz brain.

Worse than that I was beginning to like it.

CHAPTER 26. Marie Antoinette

It wasn't long after that when I found myself tied naked to a pole in the basement. All I was wearing was my SLUT collar and my clit clip with the chains that dangled teasingly over my pubes. I felt like Marie Antoinette being all trussed up at the stake for my crimes. Except Miss Antoinette probably wasn't blindfolded, she most likely didn't have a dildo gag and she certainly wasn't naked.

The twins had already paddled my bottom and the lasting sting was drawing my attention. My nipples were protruding out from between tight rope that held me firmly to the post in a most lewd approval of my position. The ladies were conversing when I heard the sound of heels approaching on the cement floor.

It had to be Miss Billingham. For just a moment I thought that the Amazon ladies may be in trouble for abusing her prized maid. I quickly found out just the opposite.

"I just wanted to check and make sure that the girl was secured. I have guests coming by and I don't want them to see the girl until she is fully trained."

"She's not going anywhere Miss Billingham. She's tied tight and I even think that at the moment she's enjoying herself."

I felt a finger flick a nipple and then insert itself between the gold jewelry chains that teased at my pubes.

"I can see that. She smells of her own sex. The girl is sopping wet. What a horny cunt she is. The bitch has been humiliated like a common street trollop and yet she is still excited for more."

I felt a finger tap my clitoris. The clit clip held it tight and made the sensation incredible. It was impossible for me to maintain any sense of dignity under such stimulation. How could I? I gave an animal sounding moan beneath my gag. They didn't seem to notice.

"Keep her shaved down there. It will increase her sexually sensitivity. I must say the girl appears to be hopelessly submissive. Isabella sure knows how to identify the subservient ones. I don't know how she does it. She has the uncanny ability to get it right each and every time. Have you put the girl through her paces yet?"

I wasn't sure if Donnie or Lonnie responded.

"Yes Miss Billingham. She's extremely submissive."

"I do hope that she has serious fetish issues. A good submissive should have a few."

"Yes Miss Billingham. We've already identified several of them. Her juices gush at the slightest hint of sexual provocation.

"Has she been put to the paddle?"

"Yes Miss Billingham. She craves the paddle."

"Does her tongue know its place?"

"We've had her lick our shoes. She does so without hesitation."

"Does she lick pussy?"

"With the best of them. She's such a slut! She laps away like a kitten at dinner. She's inexperienced but she's learning fast."

I sure that the ladies were thinking about our previous interludes. At their insistence I had pleasured them both with my tongue. There were giggles before Miss Billingham continued.

"Has she kissed ass?"

The response sounded so apologetic. How terrible — the new maid hadn't kissed ass yet!

"Sorry Miss, no not yet."

"See to it. I enjoy a good ass kissing from time to time. What about her domestic skills?"

"Extremely lacking. She seems to have no experience whatsoever when it comes to housekeeping skills. It has provided us with many opportunities — for instructional purposes of course."

The women laughed before Miss Billingham continued.

"Remember I plan on keeping this one. She has a certain innocence about her that I haven't seen before. I find it to be very attractive. But I'll not have a girl who can't keep house for me. Perfect domestic servitude is a must.

Remember the three S's. Service, submission and sex. She must be proficient in all three without compromise. These submissive girls get off on humiliation so don't be afraid to humiliate her however you can. The best way is to emphasize her position in the household. There is nothing more humiliating than the lot of a lowly whore servant. The harder you work her with domestic tasks the better. She'll no doubt enjoy it. A properly humiliated submissive will always be exceptional in bed.

I'm thinking of renaming her. Somehow Chastity just doesn't seem fitting for such a slut. What do you girls think?"

There were more giggles.

"How about Ditzy or perhaps Dilly? How about Horny? Just about anything but Virgin would do."

All three ladies laughed. It was so embarrassing I wanted to shout in protest. Instead my body betrayed me with shame when a bead of damp lust trickled down my leg. They didn't seem to notice.

"I'll give it thought. There is a certain amusing irony to Chastity. Perhaps I'll choose to keep it. Oh, I almost forgot. Is she capable of multiple orgasms? If she is to be the house harlot she must be capable of repeated orgasms."

"Yes Miss. We've had her come three times in succession."

"Train her up to four. To increase her stamina use the vibrator on her if you must but I should think she should be capable of four at the minimum. See to it."

I heard the heels of all three women walk away. I was left alone in silence with only my firm nipples and my dripping wet vagina to keep me company. The tiny chains on my clit clip continued to tease me every time I tried to wiggle free.

It would be hours before Donnie and Lonnie returned and untied me from my predicament.

CHAPTER 27. Serving Miss Billingham

It was my pleasure to tend to the needs of the lovely Miss Billingham. In the morning I did her makeup and fixed her hair. I would help her dress and then tend to her breakfast.

During the day I was engrossed in menial household tasks. I made beds, I did laundry, vacuumed, dusted, cleaned bathrooms and polished the floors. There was no end to the work that the large mansion required. At the end of the day I poured Miss Billingham a bath and helped her undress. After her bath I toweled her off and helped her into her nightgown.

I was at her service all day — and all night too. I am not ashamed to say that I was somewhat of a willing whore for the Mistress of the Manor. After all Miss Billingham was providing me with free room and board so the least that I could do was satisfy her lust in her bedroom.

Unlike the twins Miss Billingham was gentle and affectionate with me. While the twins were demanding and gruff Miss Billingham understood the delightful value of prolonged foreplay. We would cuddle and talk for hours while a lovely cloud of her perfume embraced me with a fragrant wisp of what was surely to come. Her affections would slowly seduce me out of my nightgown in preparation for a sensuous night of lovemaking.

She would start with tiny little gentle kisses on my mouth. Then her lips would make their way to my breasts where they would linger in heavenly teasing on my hardened nipples until I begged her to do much more than just that.

Finally she would tease my clitoris with the tip of her tongue while I would writhe in erotic pleasure. Just when I would approach a lusty orgasm she would stop and insist that I do the same with her.

We would repeat that sequence back and forth for hours on end while my body totally capitulated to her tantalizing advances. I never resisted Miss Billingham. I simply grew deeper and deeper into her parlor of lovemaking that was unlike anything that I had ever experienced.

After teasing me to the precipice of paradise Miss Billingham would finally get down to business with her willing maid. I had never understood the pleasure that tribbing could bring until I came vulva to vulva with her after prolonged foreplay.

I found that after our juices mixed and I humped away at my Mistress like I was a sexually deprived whore our orgasms would be simply out of this world. We would both shriek in a brazen animal lust that announced our pleasure before we would fall back in exhaustion. Then Miss Billingham would start all over again not to be satisfied until we both screamed in ecstasy once again.

Finally we would fall asleep in each other's arms. Since I was the maid I was required to wake up during the night and tip-toe out of her bedroom so that I could be prepared to offer domestic service in the morning. It took every ounce of energy to do so but the bliss that she offered me was well worth it. When I would finally settle down in my own bed I would quickly fall back to sleep content with the pleasure that our lovemaking had brought me.

That was how our love blossomed just like fresh flowers in spring.

CHAPTER 28. Ditz Brain

I would have never thought it possible to be fucked into submission. Yet at the next meeting of the tea party ladies held at Miss Billingham's mansion there I was standing at attention next to Miss Billingham holding my dress and slip up so that the ladies could witness my Sapphic Promise. Just like Deanna Travers I had truly become the ditz brain that the twins had promised to make me.

Initially I had been put to the task of serving tea. It was only after they had been properly served that Miss Billingham saw to it to show that her successful training of her new maid had produced such an obedient servant.

The ladies made no effort to hide their amusement at my dilemma. A woman who is hired as a maid and then attempts to turn a wealthy woman into a maid and succeeds at it is one thing. It is quite an achievement to be sure. But then after such success to be turned back into a maid herself is quite a humiliating accomplishment. The ladies reveled in the irony of it at my expense.

Miss Billingham was wholeheartedly congratulated for her success. At the same time I was being ridiculed for my submissive tendencies and my inability to resist them.

In a display of feminine superiority each woman took turns fondling my moist pubes and softly teasing my clitoris. Each woman commented on what a slut I was to be so aroused at such a humiliating display of my obedience. Their taunting only aroused me that much more which of course only made things worse for me. Much to the amusement of the gathering my juices flowed and glistened in a shameful display of delightful approval of my willing servitude.

I knew better than to say a word or make a movement without permission. If the Amazon ladies had taught me anything it was that swift punishment would follow any such disregard for proper protocol. I had no intention of embarrassing Miss Billingham with any sort of display of disobedience.

So I stood with my dress raised high and my slip raised up while the ladies sipped their tea and chatted amongst themselves. That was how I learned that Miss Ellsworth had sold the mansion that had previously belonged to Miss Travers and that the proceeds had been added to the fortune that had also been hers. Then the entire amount had been split among the group with Miss Ellsworth taking the largest share. She called that her finder's fee.

I learned that Deanna was still Miss Ellsworth's maid and that the group was still searching for a maid for Miss Danielle Stevens. Miss Georgette Broadworth bragged that she knew of a woman with substantial ill-gotten gains who might be the perfect candidate for the position.

I was still standing at attention with my privates fully exposed when the tea party broke up. After all of the women had left Miss Billingham told me that I was dismissed and that I could return to my room. She told me to keep my dress hiked up and my slip raised up until I entered my room and closed the door.

I passed Donnie and Lonnie in the hallway on the way to my quarters. They both giggled at the way I exposed myself and they commented how excited I appeared to be at showing them my wares.

CHAPTER 29. Sissy Boys

While I never learned the source of the lavish wealth that the ladies enjoyed I could see that they added to it by recruiting submissive girls like me and then confiscating their wealth. The twins were part of the successful scheme and that explained why they weren't always present to supervise. Apparently they also worked for the other ladies of the tea party group and similarly shared in the bounty of wealth.

While Miss Billingham didn't seem to have a need for males I did discover that the group used them for an alternative income source while they searched for submissive girls of a certain persuasion.

From time to time a female client would arrive with a shy young male in tow. The twins were always present to take charge of the new recruit. While I would serve Miss Billingham and her client lunch the twins would be busy transforming the young male.

While the ladies enjoyed their meal the young male would be transformed by the twins into a sissy maid complete with French maid uniform, apron and cap. By dinnertime the twins would emerge with the contrite young male held between them.

I saw many such transformations. Donnie and Lonnie were experts at taking a male and doing a complete makeover. As part of the transformation they would shave all the hair off the boy and then apply cosmetics, lash extensions, nail extensions and a feminine wig. By the time the sissy maid would be brought before the client she would be unrecognizable as a male.

I have no idea if Donnie and Lonnie took sexual advantage of the sissy girls. It wouldn't surprise me if they did because they were so sadistic and enjoyed such things. I do know that however they dealt with the sissy girls it was very effective. Once they treated even the most reluctant male the result was an extremely passive sissy maid.

I enjoyed watching when the sissy maid would curtsy to her Mistress and then raise up her dress for inspection. The male equivalent of my Sapphic Promise was a metal cock ring with a tiny bell attached to it that was clipped behind the sissy scrotum. All of the sissy girls that I saw must have been submissive because all of them were clearly turned on and fully aroused by such humiliation.

Once the sissy girl displayed her Sissy Promise she would be told to turn around for the ladies. It was then on the dark red bottom of the sissy that the handiwork of the twins was clearly evident. It was easy to tell how much of an objection that the sissy had put up by the size and color of the freshly spanked flesh. The deeper the hue and the more widespread the crimson was the greater the protest had been before total capitulation had been achieved.

The best part of the sissy transformations was that I would be in charge of training the sissy maid how to be a maid. I was subservient to everyone in the household including guests with the sole exception of the sissy maids.

So when there was a sissy maid in the house I would become a supervisor and my own duties would be lessened. It was fun to boss the sissy maids around while showing them the proper way to hand wash lingerie and polish floors.

Though I trained several sissy girls I never took sexual advantage of one even though Donnie told me that I was free to do so. I do know that some girls like to play games with sissy boys and I can understand that. After all sissifying a boy does make them prettier and more palatable. For those so inclined taking a lusty ride on a submissive male can be a pleasant diversion.

Still I have no taste for a sissy girl. I guess that I'm just not that kind of girl. Instead I like to treat a sissy maid like I would a novice female maid. They look cute in their maid uniforms doing all of the particularly nasty jobs while I tend to Miss Billingham myself.

The presence of a sissy maid would give me an opportunity to spend more time with Miss Billingham. She enjoyed lounging poolside in the evening watching while the sun went down. I would stand at attention just behind her waiting for instructions. The advantage point allowed me to take her bikini clad body in without her knowledge.

At times we would talk while the evening settled in. The peaceful setting allowed us to become that much closer together with our souls intertwined by the beauty of nature.

CHAPTER 30. Breaking Society Rules

We can't help but acknowledge that society attaches a stigma to Lesbian women. Those who don't understand us don't want to tolerate us. People are like that. They say they are tolerant and they are — so long as everybody is just like them.

That is why Miss Billingham had set up the perfect cover for our intimate relationship. While she gleefully indulged herself in my sexual pleasures to the outside world I was merely the maid servant who tended to Miss Billingham's other more traditional domestic needs.

All of Miss Billingham's family and friends were clearly straight. So when her friends and family visited I was simply maid Chastity at her service. For them I was a servant content to obediently tend and serve Miss Billingham's guests.

I didn't mind tending to Miss Billingham's mother, her sister, and her sorority friends along with her various business acquaintances. I realized that was my position and I was to serve faithfully with a smile on my face. I enjoyed being near attractive women and caring for their needs. Though I'm not one to complain there was however one slight embarrassing drawback.

My requirement to wear my SLUT collar always became a topic of discussion. Miss Billingham's charming Mother was her first guest to comment on seeing me wearing it. I stood nearby at attention ready to serve when she brought the issue up to Miss Billingham.

"Your maid seems to be an attractive charming young lady. Why is she wearing a collar that identifies her as a slut?"

While I would cringe at such conversation Miss Billingham seemed to revel in such an inquiry. She had a story at the ready and she relayed it to all of her guests. Yes, all of her guests inevitably asked about my collar!

"I found the maid working as a prostitute and I saved her from her fate. She is such a whore! The maid can hardly control her sexual appetite. After working hours she trolls cheap bars in search of a young lad to explore her nether regions. She hopes that the collar will entice a young man right out of his pants and into her panties. She wears it all the time in the hope a delivery boy or perhaps a groundskeeper will take note of her and satisfy her lust."

I could not think of a more humiliating explanation that Miss Billingham could have offered. It was so shameful and embarrassing that my face would often flush when hearing it. Though shamefully at the same time I found such humiliation to be pleasantly erotic.

Of course such an explanation often drew gasps from the guests. Such refined women were appalled at such a description of my sexuality. Sometimes the mere idea of a trollop in their presence was enough for them to change the subject onto other matters. I would often immediately become invisible to the person who made the inquiry. Other times I was lectured by the guests about my terrible infatuation. Perhaps Miss Billingham's Mother said it best.

"Young lady you need to control your urges. Your sex should not be given away it should be carefully guarded. A refined woman knows better than to advertise her charms like that."

If only she knew! It is an interesting commentary on society that it was easier to explain my presence as that of a partially reformed street tart than to tell the truth. Miss Billingham found it better to call me a former prostitute than to admit that I was her Lesbian lover. The world is like that. It is of no matter to me because after the guests left it was Miss Billingham that I would be passionately making love to.

You should know the truth. Of course to be clear I had no desire to be bedded by any male and I certainly had no need to troll cheap bars for sex. I was quite content with the sex that I was getting. I must admit that there was a Goth delivery girl who I fancied but I knew that I was off limits to her and that I wasn't allowed to tempt her.

Nevertheless I did on occasion generously flirt with the girl.

CHAPTER 31. A New Recruit

Months had gone by before the tea party group returned to Miss Billingham's home. I was content in my role and looking forward to a lasting relationship with Miss Billingham. The ladies were enjoying their tea and I was standing next to Miss Billingham at attention on display as her loyal servant when Lonnie and Donnie came into the room.

Lonnie was gleefully leading a woman by a leash that was attached to a collar that was around the woman's neck. The woman had bare feet that were chained together and she was covered from the neck down to her ankles with a black cape. I had a pretty good idea that she was wearing a chastity belt underneath her cape. I presumed it was a woman because even though she was blindfolded and gagged I could see her long auburn hair.

The twins stopped in front of the group of ladies who giggled at the sight of the helpless woman. Even though my head was bowed and my eyes were supposed to be lowered I couldn't help but sneak a peek at what was happening. Donnie lifted the blindfold off of the girl revealing eyes that were wild with fear. Her posture collar held her head up but with effort she was able to turn her eyes toward me. Her eyes fixed on my SLUT collar before they shifted back towards the other ladies. Miss Georgette Broadworth was smiling broadly. No doubt her new recruit had been procured and a big payday was in order for her. Miss Ellsworth spoke first.

"I see Cynthia that you've met our distinguished drivers Lonnie and Donnie. They seem to have made you quite comfortable."

The group chuckled at the girl's powerless situation. Miss Ellsworth continued.

"Forgive me dear. Perhaps introductions are in order. Ladies, please meet Miss Cynthia Hampton. She is an acquaintance of Miss Broadworth and she has been fully vetted. She comes with intimate recommendation from our colleague."

The ladies laughed at the introduction. Miss Ellsworth turned to me.

"Maid Chastity show us your Sapphic Promise. Please display yourself for Miss Hampton."

I felt so humiliated having to show myself to a new girl but I knew how important it was and I knew better than to disobey. So I hardly hesitated. I was accustomed to providing deliberate self-degradation on demand for the benefit of surprised onlookers because I had done so on many previous occasions. It would not be the first time that I felt a flush of sexual gratification from raising my skirts and exposing my restrained sex to a stunned audience. I knew that it was certain that it would not be the least time either.

I carefully lifted my dress and the plain white slip that was beneath it. Since I wasn't wearing any panties I knew that my genitals were clearly visible and that they were nicely framed by my white garter belt and the tabs holding up my stockings.

Miss Hampton's eyes fixated on my clitoris and on the golden clit clip with the tiny golden jewelry chains that dangled down over my vulva. I swayed my hips slightly so that the strands of the chain gently teased me with a blissful caress that I had come to desire. The movement caused me to imagine myself lost in a far-away world where I was being pleasured by Miss Billingham in her bed.

Miss Ellsworth continued.

"My dear Miss Hampton this leaves you with quite the dilemma. As you see Miss Belden is wearing a clit clip as a sign of her total surrender of her body to Miss Billingham. She has such a pretty clitty doesn't she? You may notice that she is wet with desire just holding herself so shamelessly for our amusement. She was once just like you but now she is a submissive maid servant. She does the bidding of Miss Billingham both in and out of her bedroom. You may notice her SLUT collar. It is quite descriptive of her I can assure you.

I believe that you have the same desirable potential as Miss Belden. Miss Broadworth assures us that you have similar submissive qualities and similar desires for female companionship. You may surrender your body today and become a maid as well or I can turn you over to the police. We know all about the little game that you are playing with company money. Such illegal activities from such a pretty girl! You should know better than to do that. Shame, shame! Nevertheless we are benevolent enough to give you a choice. It is your decision to determine how we should proceed.

I can assure you that if you turn down your opportunity to serve as a willing maid that charges will be pressed and that you will spend the rest of your life in jail tending to the sexual needs of other female prisoners. That would be such a terrible fate for such a lovely girl. What will it be?"

The girl tried to speak but the penis gag prevented anything other than a muffled murmur of a sound. The ladies laughed at her inability to speak before Miss Ellsworth continued.

"We'll take that to be a yes. Oh did I mention that I've arranged a little amusement here for your benefit? Ladies please give me your sealed bids."

The ladies each gave a white envelope to Miss Ellsworth. Miss Ellsworth began to open them up one at a time while building suspense with each succeeding envelope.

"Miss Hampton you should know that you are in high demand. The first two bids are quite substantial. Miss Jones is out of the running and right now you stand to be the property of Miss Beverly Hinton."

She opened another envelope.

"Oh Georgette you bested Beverly and you are in the lead!"

She opened another envelope.

"Sorry Georgette, you didn't make the cut and Danielle is now high bid."

The final envelope belonged to Miss Billingham. I was concerned that Miss Billingham would be sharing her bed with another woman. I wasn't sure that I would be able to handle that. What would become of me? Since I hadn't been instructed to lower my dress I was still holding my dress up exposing my clit clip while I held my breath. Miss Ellsworth opened the envelope.

"Congratulations Danielle you are now the proud owner of maid Cynthia."

The ladies all applauded the winner. Miss Ellsworth handed a golden key to Miss Danielle which I knew went to the chastity belt that was no doubt secured beneath Cynthia's cape. Miss Danielle motioned and Donnie came forward. Miss Danielle handed her the key.

"Take her to my estate and prepare her properly. Make her a platinum blonde and style that hair into something more suitable for a working maid.

142

Long hair like what she has will only get in the way in the bedroom so there is no point to it. I'll be home in a few hours to take possession of her."

"Yes Miss Stevens."

With that the girl's blindfold was put back in place and Lonnie and Donnie led her out of view. I smiled. I knew the fate that awaited Miss Cynthia Hampton. She would make the Sapphic Promise. She would become a domestic maid. She would have her brains fucked out and she would be turned into a ditz brain. Then she would spend her life having blissful Lesbian sex with her new Mistress.

It is the dream of every girl who makes the Sapphic Promise. Just like me.

About The Author

Lisa Rose Farrow is a successful business woman who enjoys sharing her dominant lifestyle through her imaginative works of literature. Her writing is inspired by her real world experiences with her dominant female friends and their submissive males and their submissive females.

Ms. Farrow believes that a strong household begins with a strong woman and that in business women possess far better leadership skills than men. Her playful imaginative S&M works extol and emphasize the superior role of dominant women in both business and pleasure. She also enjoys exposing the erotic allure of female sexual submission.

When she is not at work Ms. Farrow appreciates attending the symphony and touring art museums.

"There are those who might call me a tease and they would certainly be right about that. I take pride in knowing that I can entertain and tantalize with my writing. There is nothing wrong with being a temptress."

Dominant females, submissive males and submissive females and all will enjoy Lisa's erotic stories.

Ms. Farrow's saucy titles include *The Maid's Maid*, *The Maid's Fury*, *Sonja Says*, *Miss Sadie's Salon*, *Trophy Maid*, *Super Model Maid*, *The Legend of Connie Swisher*, *Yes Miss Margo*, *Sissy Recruiter*, *My Sister's Sissy Maid*, *Bitches of Birchwood*, *Sissy Maid Wives Club*, *Sissy Glamour Shots* and *The Sapphic Diary*.

THE DELICIOUSLY EROTIC WORLD OF LISA ROSE FARROW

Enjoy all of the tempting pleasures that the deliciously erotic world of Lisa Rose Farrow has to offer you!

Sissy Glamour Shots
by Lisa Rose Farrow
Link: http://a.co/d/aigrrfw

In *Sissy Glamour Shots* Lisa gets an opportunity to work with her friend Heather and to put things straight with her misbehaving male supervisor — an errant manager named Brendan. You'll find out that things turn out quite differently than usual for Heather when Brendan is taught an unforgettable lesson.

Sissy Maid Wives Club: Girls Having Fun
by Lisa Rose Farrow
Link: http://a.co/0GX5Obe

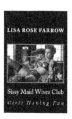

When Lisa begins to have issues with her husband she consults her good friend and marriage counselor extraordinaire Pamela Sinclair. When Pamela divulges her secret to successful marriages Lisa joins in the fun and soon her husband is transformed into her own sissy maid. Sissy Maid Wives Club is a charming romp through gender transformation that will leave you begging for more! Taking control of males is unbelievably easy if you know how to do it.

Bitches Of Birchwood: A Sissy Maid Lesson
by Lisa Rose Farrow
Link: https://a.co/1eH8y9S

The *Bitches of Birchwood* are sexy female cops who just happen to be female supremacists. With their special brand of law enforcement they offer the city of Birchwood the absolute ultimate in feminine protection. Lisa's bed and breakfast receives a boost when the all-female special crimes unit decides to relocated their command center to her country inn. Her world is then turned upside down after she accepts an offer to participate in a stakeout with the authoritative police women.

Her disrespectful boyfriend Phillip doesn't believe Lisa when she describes the events that took place on the stakeout. You'll root for the long arm of the law when Phillip is taught a sissy girl lesson that he will never forget by the ruthless *Bitches of Birchwood*.

My Sister's Sissy Maid: Taming A Wandering Spouse
by Lisa Rose Farrow
Link: https://amzn.com/B01J4ZCWPC

When Professor Cora suspects her husband Blaine of infidelity she decides to have her sister Lindsay keep an eye on both her house and her husband for her while she is abroad. Cora's suspicions turn out to be accurate when Lindsay finds Blaine seemingly has more than a casual interest in college coeds.

Lindsay realizes that she will be alone with Blaine for months until Cora returns. What should Lindsay do with her sister's straying husband? Is there a maid uniform in his future? What about those college coeds? Big sisters always know best and Blaine will quickly discover that first hand.

Sissy Recruiter: Entrapment
by Lisa Rose Farrow
Link: https://amzn.com/B01ESAXJXC

Authoritative women always get what they want. When they want an adoring sissy girl they come to The Ellington Agency and ask for Sierra Ellington—the sissy recruiter. Take a trip into the sexy world of sissy recruiting where women choose sissy girls like they are from a catalog and The Ellington Agency delivers them just like they are ordered.

You'll feel the excitement of recruiting when case studies of sissy maids, sissy secretaries and sissy nurses are all shared. Then you'll share the thrill of transformation! What kind of woman orders a sissy girl? What kind of sissy accepts such an invitation? You'll feel the heat when you explore the world of sissy recruiting!

Yes Miss Margo: A Sissy Maid Transformation
by Lisa Rose Farrow
Link: https://amzn.com/B015VIAIYS

Margo Farnswell married her husband Richard after a quick whirlwind romance. It turned out to be the mistake of her life. She tolerated his treatment of her until she couldn't take it anymore.

What is it like to incur the wrath of a woman scorned? Will Margo escape from Richard? Will her scheme for revenge work? Is it the ultimate punishment for a cheating husband to be turned into a passive sissy maid? Find out for yourself in this erotic tale of sissy maid transformation that will leave you begging for the attention of a Dominant Woman.

The Legend of Connie Swisher: Sissy Maid Servitude
by Lisa Rose Farrow
Link: https://amzn.com/B010GSOA4W

Jennifer Banks enjoyed her position as a college instructress until she was let go due to an unfortunate incident with a male student. Blacklisted and unable to find employment Jennifer jumped at the chance to interview at Chardin College for Women though she knew little about the history of the college.

She is surprised by what she finds on campus. The campus that was built during the Civil War has remained a place out of time complete with a lack of electricity and Victorian maid service.

Jennifer's erotic adventure begins when she hears of the legend of Connie Swisher--the woman who founded the college. Could it be true that at Chardin young girls are taught to train and to dominate submissive males? How will Jennifer deal with haughty female professors? You'll

discover all of the sensual secrets of Chardin
College for Women right along with Jennifer as
she explores the hidden side of Chardin College
for Women.

Previously the secrets of venerable Chardin
College were known only to the staff and
graduates. For the first time ever the tawdry past
is revealed. Is it possible that males are actually
present on the all-woman campus? If so where
are they hidden?

Enter the world of Chardin College where
women rule and males are trained to serve them.
Entertaining erotic adventure awaits you on the
campus of Chardin College whether you are
Dominant Woman enough to seek pleasure there
or a willing sissy maid eager to provide service.

Super Model Maid: The Humiliation Of Charlotte Prentiss

by Lisa Rose Farrow

Link: https://amzn.com/B00OO8M2JQ

Charlotte Prentiss has enjoyed her life as a famous super model. If only she could have Terrence Covington as her adoring husband her life would be perfect. But to her dismay the wealthy Terrence pays no attention to her charming looks. So with her modeling agent she plots a scheme to gain the attention of Terrence by working as his domestic maid. Things don't go exactly as planned and when Charlotte discovers her submissive side she finds out that becoming a domestic maid involves much more than she bargained for.

In *Super Model Maid* you'll enjoy the erotic humiliation of Charlotte Prentiss as she tumbles down the social ladder. Her life as a super model fades away to be replaced by that of a mere maid. Will she be able to overcome her own feelings

---

and get her high fashion life back or will she succumb to her intense erotic desire to serve?

If you have sexual submissive feelings of your own you'll enjoy this enticing lady to maid transformation. Be careful what you wish for!

Trophy Maid: The Humiliation Of Elizabeth Bennington
by Lisa Rose Farrow
Link: https://amzn.com/B00KPJ7XZ6

Elizabeth Bennington is a rich socialite enjoying a fine life of luxury. When things go awry she finds herself in an unfamiliar situation — penniless with no place to live. Under the circumstances and with no other option she accepts a position working for her former maid Marlene Holloway. How will Marlene treat Elizabeth? Can a rich socialite actually become a maid?

In Trophy Maid Lady Lisa Rose Farrow explores every working maid's fantasy — turning her employer into her own maid! At the same time she delves deeply into sexual humiliation as Elizabeth Bennington is taught the ultimate lesson in humility as she tumbles down the social ladder into a life of domestic servitude.

Miss Sadie's Salon
by Lady Lisa Rose Farrow
Link: https://amzn.com/B00GU1J6GC

Together Miss Sadie with Miss Mattie—the back
seam girls—own Miss Sadie's salon. A sissy
maid adventure begins when a naive young male
innocently applies for a position at the salon.
Will he become a back seam girl too? In Miss
Sadie's Salon the reader is skillfully teased and
denied as you are seduced right along with Miss
Sadie into an S/M adventure that will leave you
breathless.

Will Miss Sadie's desire for her new sissy
employee lead her to fulfillment or to something
else? Is Miss Sadie dominant or submissive? Can
she possibly be both? In this explicit novel you'll
writhe in pleasure right along with Miss Sadie
and her newly hired sissy maid as you experience
the power of domination interwoven with the
thrill of submission.

Sonja Says: Women Rule!
by Lady Lisa Rose Farrow
Link: https://amzn.com/B00C52CC84

In *Sonja Says* you will delight in seeing the dominant side of superior women as Lady Lisa Rose Farrow intimately describes the experience of her good friend Sonja Blake. Relish this erotic submissive cross dressing account by Lady Lisa Rose Farrow as she shares the ascent of her friend Sonja Blake from unappreciated secretary to dominant businesswoman. You'll be amused with how Sonja dealt with the sexual urges of an irreverent male who owned the maid service where she worked.

Any woman who has ever worked for an impertinent male will savor this titillating story. You will feel the thrill of female superiority as you discover what happens to Preston—Sonja's former boss--who treats women employees with nothing but disrespect. You'll be wonderfully entertained as Sonja systematically puts him in his place after she discovers his innermost secret.

There is nothing like enjoying the futile struggle of a helpless male who can't resist his urge to serve a superior woman. What happens to Preston when the tables are turned? Is Preston sissy enough to fill her heels?

Cross-dressing submissive males beware. Dominant women can be found in places you would never expect and there is a fine line between secretly cross-dressing yourself and becoming a permanent sissy maid. Coming out of the closet is one thing—being pulled out is quite another. If you enjoy submitting to authoritative women or you simply need to be put in your place then this is required reading for you. *Sonja Says*--you will obey!

The Maid's Fury
by Lady Lisa Rose Farrow
Link:

Enjoy the lure of female supremacy in the erotic novels of Lady Lisa Rose Farrow. Explore the taboo sensations of revenge, lust, as well as a world of cross dressing, Femdom, and bondage. Lady Farrow indulges her reader in a blend of erotic Femdom reality and erotic S/M fantasy that is her trademark. Drawing on her own experiences Lady Lisa Rose details a life of feminine superiority that leaves superior women satisfied and sissy males pining for conquest.

Of course when Lisa Farrow is around submission is always demanded, expected, and encouraged. In the continuation of her novel The *Maids Maid* you'll learn what happens to maid Sheila and maid Nora. In a final confrontation with Lady Camilla you'll be surprised at the outcome as the full fury of a dominant woman is unleashed. Return with Lady Lisa Rose Farrow back to a place of decadent feminine superiority in *The Maid's Fury*.

The Maid's Maid
by Lady Lisa Rose Farrow
Link: https://amzn.com/B0085ZCTLA

A lady scorned, a rich Aunt, a secret society of dominant women, and a large estate in need of servants all await Lisa Rose Farrow's would be beau. In this scintillating S/M erotica adventure you'll find out what happens when the needs of a submissive cross-dresser meet the fury of a spurned woman who is in a position to control his every action.

Lisa Rose Farrow takes revenge for every woman who has ever waited in vain for that special guy to ask her out. After high school graduation her path crosses again with Charles — the object of her unrequited love. She finds that she is now over him but it is payback time for Charles when she discovers his submissive side.

Tutored by her Aunt Millie while working as her maid, Lisa Rose has become an expert Dominatrix and now spares no mercy taking out her frustrations on hapless Charles!

Printed in Great Britain
by Amazon